Contact the author: brian@briandgarrity.com

Or

Visit: www.briandgarrity.com

Cover design: Simon Melroy

Author photo: Craig Perman

Cover photo: Brian D Garrity   Model and Styling: Trixie

'What monstrosities would walk the streets were some people's faces as unfinished as their minds' - Eric Hoffer

'I don't know a lot, but I know more'n alotta people I know' - anonymous

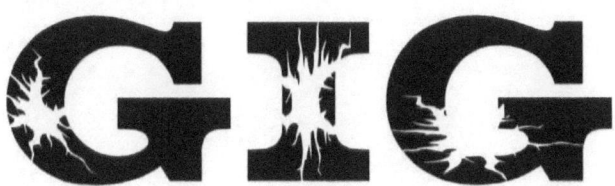

KATIE

The dream had been bad, really bad.

It began as usual. Katie was painting in a large, very beautiful Victorian manor. Soft spring sunlight pulsed through elegantly leaded bay windows, throwing vague little rainbows into the peripherals of the room.

The light here, from the windows seemed to be
Perfect.

Yes, it was.

The painting

She looked at the painting. Watched with interest, her hands doing intimate little dances with the brush and paint she had never before conceptualized. The tones were alive, the composition and execution were

The face

Perfect.

She looked at the face. It was a portrait of a handsome young man. He was standing on a stage holding some strange manner of instrument in his hands. There was something about the way he stared out at you through the canvas. Something old and familiar, but something yet unseen. His eyes were

Wild

Alive.

He smiled at her.

What's wrong with this picture?

She stifled a giggle. Pictures didn't smile. But here he was and wasn't that a peculiar device he held and the way the light crawled around in the back of his eyes while he touched her hand feeling the object pressed against her back while they kissed only it wasn't an instrument and the way he put it to his lips and said

"My mother, my lover, I have something for you."

His smile and that sound.

ABYSS

Bill noticed the beer in his hand.

A cool spring breeze slid up the sheer cliff, playing with his hair. He took a deep breath of arid vegetation rising from the valley below and slapped the can into place over his mouth. Flat, stale beer rushed down his throat, effectively eliminating any accompanying flavors or fragrances. He held this gesture till the can surrendered its contents. Outliving its usefulness, it dove to the dirt beside a growing number of its peers.

Bill glanced over at Mark. Mark was sitting on the precipice beside him, dangling legs over the 250 foot drop, shoulders hunched, one hand holding up his head. He looked like The Thinker. Mark noticed his glance; rediscovered his own beer.

Belching loudly, Bill sent it echoing out across the valley, not even provoking a response from Mark. Usually he'd either fly off on what a fucking slob he was, or try to outdo Bill with one of his own. The valley swallowed up the echo's, puffing fresh air back into their faces. They both were silent.

Bill was almost startled by Mark's voice.

"It's so damned beautiful here. You know, I've always come to this spot when shit went wrong, or I just wanted to get away. Up here, you can… I dunno, stand back a little. See the order…the complexity of things. Structures. You believe that there's got to be some purpose for all this mess." He snickered, then grew intent on the valley below, all the small, subtle events happening there.

Mark's voice changed.

"God. It's so sad. It's so fucking sad."

For a moment, Bill felt the current grab him; a tsunami of thoughts and emotions threatening to pull him into the soundless void, a vacuum holding a huge black nothing. A place he'd visited last night. Willing himself up against the buffeting darkness, he returned to his body on the bluff.

"I cried all night. Like a little kid."

"I can't cry any more. Don't do no good."

Mark fought with his hair.

"I read somewhere that traumatic experiences can speed the metabolism up, can actually make your hair grow."

Bill looked wildly at Mark; expectantly.

"Think mine's grown about a foot since yesterday."

Bill shook his head, inwardly glad at Mark's attempt at humor.

"I think you read too much."

"I think you think too much."

Bill's mind shifted. He saw the image of a beautiful young woman. A woman with whom he had shared some of the fullest moments of his life. Icy fingers clutched his stomach, tearing it down through his bowels.

"Shelly's dead. I don't want to believe it. Shit…talked to her about an hour before it happened." He took a deep breath. "Heard stories of people who get, like, a hand severed in an accident, and for a long time they actually still feel it there. Feel it move, feel pain. Phantom hand. How I feel about Shell's. And Dan, and Pete. They're still here. I can feel them. They're so close."

Mark talked to the abyss.

"Long as we remember them, they live with us. You believe in parallel realities?"

Bill shook his head. "Don't know."

"Yeah…not sure what I believe in anymore. Things are so different. It's all changed." Shifting his gaze from the valley, Mark faced Bill, eyes piercing his, eyes that perceived beyond, ancient, but then he broke first, looking south, down the river, where it lazily blurred with the horizon. Mark's voice barely above a whisper.

"Do you know how it happened; the accident?"

"Just what the papers reported. They said-"

Mark turned back, vehement.

"Fuck the goddamn papers and their sensationalist bullshit! The papers said that there was beer involved. Sure there was beer involved; a twelve-pack on the floor. Unopened."

Bill controlled his tone.

"I thought you couldn't remember anything."

"I lied. I didn't want to talk about it. Lying changes reality. The papers change reality." Mark's voice went low again.

"He tried to race the train. It was a big joke. A big

fucking joke. Christ; he was still laughing when it hit."
Mark smashed his beer down in disgust, the half-full can
gurgling it's contents cheerfully out onto the stone,
mocking him.

Bill was taken aback. He'd not heard the details.
The shocking stupidity of it all. He couldn't think of
anything to say; Mark was beginning to scare him.
Looking at Mark's squashed can, he thought of Dan's
Mustang.

"I'll grab you another."

Bill stood a little unsteadily, feeling his head spin,
and briefly questioned the sanity of getting drunk on a
cliffside. He'd nearly stepped off the face. Mark shot him
a glance telling him his joke was not appreciated.
Shrugging it off, he shuffled his way to a monumental
splinter of stone jutting up at such an angle as to suggest
it having been dropped there from a great height.

The beer waited inside a cool crevasse. Bill was
surprised to find over half the case had vanished. He
dipped a hand into the box pulling out two cold cans.
Moisture had condensed on their sides, and he put one to
his face, feeling the burn in his cheeks and forehead
slowly subside.

Light splashed over the side of the stone, revealing myriad declarations of love, initials, proclamations, and marijuana leaves that had been scribed in the soft sandstone over the years. His free hand fingered a particularly deep etch, sending tiny rivulets of sand onto his feet and into the case.

"Hey, here's Pete's initials. Remember…do you remember the night he did that? Gotta be about three years ago. Shit, that was the first time Shelly and I went out."

"Before he stole her from you." Mark's voice from somewhere behind.

"Yeah…rat bastard." As it turned out, they'd made a better couple. They'd all remained friends. "You know, Pete is the only guy in the world who corrects the spelling of his own name on bathroom graffiti."

He stopped. "Was."

He heard Mark groan. "Poor Pete…shit…"

Bill made his way back and plopped a beer before him. Mark started to rock forward, stopping suddenly. He stayed that way for a long time. Bill was starting to become concerned when a low chuckle convulsed his crouched body. It wasn't a happy sound.

Shifting his weight sideways, he looked at Mark. "What. What's so funny?" He didn't like the sound of that laughter.

Mark grew silent again, slowly drawing his drooping head up to look at Bill. His head was cocked, one eyebrow perched high on his forehead, giving his face a more angular, intelligent look than usual.

"Know what the last thing Pete said was?" A peculiar gleam haunted his eyes. The corner of his mouth twitched.

A chill rode Bill's spine. He fumbled for something to say. "Uh…no. What?"

The twitch turned to a grin and Mark screamed.

"Aaaaaaauuuugh!" He stared through Bill with wild eyes and the scream became a hysterical cackle. Flopping backwards onto the stone, he lay on his back, laughter dwindling. Setting the beer on his stomach, he was silent again.

The hair on Bill's neck decided to lay back down; he took a short gulp of air. The adrenaline flushed his system, and he felt blood drain from his brain to wherever it normally went.

"Shit. Man…don't do that again."

"Sorry." Mark sighed.

The sun was slowly sliding down to kiss the ridges on the far side of the abyss, turning the valley, and the cliffs behind, a fiery orange. Bill looked to it, feeling it's warmth embrace him, focusing on it's brightness, it's pureness, letting thoughts clear, and mind drift, encompassing an empty fullness. Time was death, life merely interrupting time, forcing it to plod in a singular direction. Death was a process of returning time to its relative state.

Opening his eyes, Bill was surprised to find the sun a flattened red orb squatting on the horizon.

"Suns going down. How long we been here?"

Mark, still lying on his back, staring at the darkening sky, pulled his wrist up; considered the bright band of skin there that bisected his tanned arm. He glanced over at the pile of mutilated beer cans.

"About a case."

"We should get back before dark."

"Yeah."

Bill felt a familiar presence in his bladder.

"Shit, nature calls."

As a precaution, he crabbed away from the edge

before tackling the now-demanding job of standing. Still, he managed to misjudge some shallow depressions in the rock floor enough to cause concern; he was driving.

Mark called from his vigil as Bill weaved his way between the strewn boulders.

"Hey, you know...Bill? You know why I think this happened? We're midwest. Middle class. Middle of the road, man. Reality is thinnest in the middle. Read that somewhere."

Bill settled in front of a small outcropping. "That doesn't make any sense. Think you read too much."

Urine spattering dangerously close to his shoes, Bill pondered upon the need for males to piss onto an object; a tree, rock, a wall. He could just as easily have peed off the cliff. No, wait. Bad idea, that.

Abruptly his thoughts were cut off. A wave rolled though his mind, invisibly churning the air about. The rocks dissolved then reformed beneath his feet. Pressure seemed impossibly high, and he waited, feeling it abate.

Clumsily buckling his belt, Bill walked around the corner to where he and Mark had spent the better part of a day.

Blood roared in his ears. A numbness settled over

his face, spreading to his fingertips.

On the ledge sat two lonely beer cans silently watching over the city.

Mark was gone.

"Mark?" But he thought he might already know.

Apprehensively approaching the edge, Bill peered into the abyss.

No body.

He watched his foot kick (Mark's) beer can, followed it's twisting descent before it smacked satisfyingly onto a ledge near the bottom, spraying the tree-line below with a fine mist of malt.

Beer rain.

Bill made his way up the path leading to the parking lot in a stupor, distractedly picking up empties. Numbness cocooned him; things began to fall out of context, the damaged timeline of a poorly edited film.

The radio was on, the vapidly familiar station identification washing over him. He was in his car following the narrow switchback road that hugged the side of the bluff.

Mark was...

Something caught his attention; he snapped back

into the moment.

The radio.

"… that tragic accident last night that took the lives of three Central High students, has now claimed a fourth. The car-train collision occurred at approximately 10:45 pm at the foot of Grandad's bluff as the vehicle the students were in apparently tried to out-race a southbound Burlington Northern through active signals. Apparently, there was alcohol involved. The victims; seventeen year old Shelly Forer, nineteen year old Dan Thomas, and eighteen year old Peter Huber all died on arrival. The sole survivor of that devastating incident, eighteen year old Mark Weisman, succumbed to multiple injuries today at approximately 4:00 pm.

"I would like to dedicate this song to them…"

A saccharine pop song cut in. Bill's hand snapped off the radio. Nausea overcame him and the road doubled, then tripled before the car. His head throbbed with what was turning out to be a hangover, and his stomach did a couple of slow turns. He was going to be sick.

Bill pulled over to the side of the road.

JORRY'S WALK

Jorry was walking downtown again, buffeted by cold, hard winds, thoughts clattering around his mind like crushed ice in a tin bucket. Thoughts about the train-wreck his life had become.

Tailspin.

The word kept appearing over the brittle shards of his thoughts. Tight fucking tailspin, too.

There was the job- really, more the lack of one. A lifelong investment in a career in photography that had pretty much had gone the way of the Dodo.

Digital.

A paradigm shift in technology, and now, with acumen for social media, and money in the right place, anyone could be a pro. Voices spoke in his head.

"Hey look honey, I just point and click, stick this motherfucking card into the reader, point and click again. Presto! I could be Ansel Adams."

"Well darling, if you like that, check this out. Ansel Adams software! Just point and click. Look at that! Even better than fucking Ansel Adams!"

He drew a twelve gauge and blew both their brains to a wet smear on the far wall of his mind.

A gust blasted down from the surrounding high-rises, nearly pushing Jorry into moving traffic. Another conversation surfaced in his mind.

"Oh yeah, there's the debacle of your love-life, that somehow got tangled with the housing situation. How's that going?"

Never go back, he would've told anyone in his situation, but there was no one to tell him, and of course he'd gone back. And naturally, she'd taken the other prick back less than a month later.

Tailspin. A helical spiral that turns in upon itself.

Starting across an intersection, a bus blew the light, hissing, brakes screaming, narrowly missing him. Jorry mentally grabbed the prick and threw him beneath the leviathan's front wheel wells, watching with satisfaction as he was ground up into bright hamburger.

Approaching the opposite side, he noticed a pigeon hopping, scuttling from street to sidewalk, and back again.

"Stupid bird, gonna' get yourself killed."

It turned and he saw nearly half its head was torn open, raw red flesh surrounding tuft of feather, wet piece of brain peeking from tiny shattered skull. It convulsed drunkenly against the curb.

"Bird, you're all fucked up."

He felt the tailspin curl tighter.

"Bird, you look how I feel."

GODLESS

"So I gotta take a leak at the Tizzzle Rizzle, *yo?* 'Cause of the beer? Get in the can and zip down, pull it out an' just then I notice this guy sittin' on the shitter right there next to me, just sorta looks up an' says *'hey'*, there's no, like, divider or anything, see? Just me, dick in hand, and the dude next to me, drop-pantsed, shit-farting into a toilet bowl that scares the hell outta me even with *my* pants on, an' suddenly I gotta piss so bad that I can't fuckin' pee. *Jesus*, I mean, I'm smellin' this guy's shit comin' outta his asshole in *real time*, an' it's got my cock short-circuited. That shit ever happen to *you?*"

Barris fingers the trigger-guard, then the trigger of the Kalashnikov in his hands, feeling his appendage come away sticky from the hot metal surface. Probably beer from the party last night, but *Christ,* when was the last time he checked the action?

Racking the bolt back by hand, he chambers another round as an unspent cartridge spits out the breech and tinkles to the concrete at his feet.

"The fuck, man, ..." Hondo unshoulders the unwieldy RPG he'd been balancing there, and making sure the sinister projectile points skyward, jerks his head at the round still rolling around on the ground, "...you think ammo grows on, ...on, ..." His fingers scratch through thick muttonchops. "...trees?"

"Like you'd know what a tree was." Barris bends and picks the thing up, holding the casing, and raps the bullet-tip, ringed in black to indicate an armor-piercing round, off his front teeth. "I don't drop a note, and I never waste a round." He slips it into one of the multitude of pockets on his camo's. "Savin' this for something special."

"Trees' one of those fuzzy green things." Hondo grunts, adjusting the heavy backpack, cradling the rocket launcher between his neck and shoulder. He squints against the setting sun down the street at the massive twin overpasses of the Interstate that glitters in a syncopated rhythm from the fractalized reflections of countless passing windshields. He checks his watch. "When's this thing gonna go down, anyway?"

Barris presses at something clipped to his ear. "Hey Ray, we got an ETA on the ball here?" He makes a face and rolls his eyes. "Christ Ray, we're sittin' here with our ordnance hanging out for all to see." He sighs, throwing his arm out, notices the Kalashnikov there, and quickly pulls it back in, ducking a little. "Yeah, yeah. We *are* concealed, but an RPG ain't like stashing a cigarette, you know?"

Eyeing the T-Rock Bar kitty-corner from their position, Hondo swallows dryly watching Barris sign off the ear-thing. "What's she say?"

"She's at Gamma Station with a clear sightline four clicks down the highway. Nothing yet."

"Well fuck ..." Hondo sets the RPG under the smashed wheel-well of the bullet ridden tour bus' hulk they were positioned behind. "... I'm getting a drink."

Barris glares at him. "Yeah, that's a *great* idea."

"It's just across the street." Hondo's already working his way though the traffic. "It's freakin' hot out here."

"Four minutes! And don't piss off the Goose! He got us that gig next week!" But Hondo's on the other side of the street, out of earshot.

The Triple Rock Social Cub wavers over the broken sidewalk, its battered, peeling exterior striated by countless layers of posters and graffiti tags, testament to generations of displaced souls that had briefly called this club home.

The interior of the bar is cool and dark, with only a few choked rays of sunlight pushing through small, high-set windows on one wall. In contrast, the bottom-lit bottles behind the bar throw up inviting rainbowed hues, and the jukebox crashes out an old 'Naked Raygun' song. A few daytime regulars sit hunched over drinks, the Day-Glo colors of their spiked and mohawked hair interspersed with patches of gray, facial piercings tarnished and drooping, leather jackets cracked and peeling.

Goose is a large barrel-shaped man with thick Buddy Holly glasses and a week or two of scrubby stubble covering his face. He comes out from behind the counter and greets Hondo wearing a 'Free The Memphis Three' T-shirt. Something of a personal affectation, he always wore shirts emblazoned with arcane meanings that nobody but Goose, presumably, understood.

"Hey, Hondo,..." He bellows. "... something cold for you?"

"Yeah, Goose. Chilled Jagermeister."

"Excellent." He bends to work the machine, sets a frosted shot-glass filled with dark liquor on the bar. *"Dee-licious!"*

"Thanks Goose." He tosses a few bills on the counter, making sure an ample tip is included.

"Whatcha doin' in the hood, Hondo? Gig isn't till Tuesday."

Hondo checks his watch and throws back the shot. "Big game at the new stadium today." He coughs, feeling the Jagermeister hitting home. "We're pre-empting it."

Goose's eyes narrow through the thick glasses. "Awww, you fuckers aren't hitting the overpass again, are you?"

"Goose, it's symbolic. They worship a ball."

"They worship the game."

"Yeah, yeah, yeah. Same difference."

Goose pulls himself up to his full height, dwarfing Hondo, and points to one of the slatted openings in the wall, this one covered by a crudely cut piece of plywood. "Remember your last I-94 excursion?"

"They have that new composite glass, you know, ..."

"You want the drink prices to go up?"

Hondo checks his watch again. "No worries, see? We're hitting it from the other side." He lied. "Gotta go."

"You better be fuckin' careful. I mean it Hon." Goose growls.

"Yeah, yeah, yeah. See you Tuesday." He pushes out the door, the heat and light hitting him like a hammer, and he sees Barris waving to him from across the street.

"Two minutes, yo! Flame-on!" He holds the AK-47 at the ready as Hondo preps the RPG.

"So what happened?"

"What?"

"Dude in the can."

"Oh, yeah. Punched him out."

Hondo looks back incredulously, flipping the little sight up. "You punched out some poor guy on the crapper? Kinda harsh, y'think?"

"Well, yeah, had to." Barris gives the banana-clip a tap to make sure it's seated properly. "Was in the middle of our set. Remember when I left the stage between 'Yakuza Girl' and 'War Babies'?"

"Oh. So that's where you went."

"Show must go on."

"True 'an true, 'mon." Hondo levers the RPG back on his shoulder, pointing it through the heat-warped frame of the passenger door's window.

Barris presses the ear-thing. "Ray. Ray, yeah. OK. Yeah, OK, yeah, OK, copy." Eyeing Hondo. "T-minus fifty-five seconds, ...mark."

Thumbing the safety-lever, Hondo takes careful aim at the intersection of the highway bed and its support column. "Thing better work. This package wasn't designed for a structure hit."

"Dante's new recipe. He guarantees results." Barris pulls a pair of high-res Zeiss binoc's out of his back pocket, snaps them open, and, leaning out from behind the wreck's grill, goggles down the highway. "Umm, ... wait for my signal. Lookin' for a break. Much as I want to send these Godfuckers back to their maker, gotta keep the collateral down."

Hondo feels the edge come on, its sharp blade honed slightly by the neutralizing effects of the Jagg. "Window time, Barris."

"Got a break coming. Ready Hon?"

"Righteously, motherfucker." He is breathing calm, his

whole being centered around where the sights meet their intended target. Hands rock-steady.

Barris is poised against the grill, still goggling, the rifle coming up in an unconscious gesture. "On three, ..."

"Wait, ...is that 4/4 or,..."

"*Jesus*, ...one,"

"Two."

"Three."

Hondo squeezes the trigger and the rocket jumps out of the tube with a shushing sound, its backflash burning an abandoned bus-stop kiosk, the projectile floating on a fat thread of its own exhaust toward the overpass, where, perhaps, an upward thermal thwarts its course. It glances off the top railing and spirals slowly into an upper-income high-rise project under construction, charge detonating with a bright flash about halfway through. The building trembles, then the southern half of the structure crumbles in slow motion, gray against the sunset.

The delayed thump of the sound-wave hits them.

"Hey man, nice shot."

"No worries,..." Reaching into his backpack, Hondo pulls out the cylinder of the backup rocket, "...it's serendipity. Those Zuppy condo's truly needed some urban renewal, ..."

The bus lurches and the world explodes in a hailstorm of light and sound.

Barris and Hondo reflexively duck, each behind one of the bus' heavy axles as the thing's exoskeleton shreds and actually *tears* outwards in a rapid series of small sonic booms. A torrent of molten metal sparks crackle through the air around them, hissing into the moist grass, clanging off a street sign in a tempo that Barris notes, and the frame of the big bus heaves a metallic sigh, its center collapsing to the pavement, sloppily bisected.

The fusillade ceases, and, ears ringing against the abrupt silence, Hondo sees Barris screaming into the ear-thing.

"Cocksucking shitsreaming Jesus, Ray! Yeah, *I see 'em!"* Body twitching wildly as he tries to peer around the smoldering wreck, Barris is looking a little hysterical and Hondo realizes that he's got his own Sig-Saur 9-mm out, locked and loaded. "Yeah, one, ...no, ...two Centurion patrols directly beneath the overpass, and they got a fuckin' *Gatling* on top a Humvee." He gestures at Hondo. "I dunno. Twenty-millimeter?"

"Nah. Fifty-cal. Twenty would've chewed through the hubs." Hondo chances a glance beneath the undercarriage, pistol in his hand feeling like a pea-shooter, and sure enough, there are two patrol cars lurking behind concrete pylons and the Humvee, standing brazenly in the center of the road, multiple barrels of the Gatling gun a metallic mandala pointed dead-on at them. On the side of the Hummer is painted the logo of the National Church of Athletics, a baroque golden Teutonic cross, orbited by the stylized symbols of a basketball, baseball, football, and a hockey puck.

Then he sees something that immediately freezes his bowels.

"*Ah, fuck.*" He turns to Barris, who is still talking.

"...pinned down. Ray. I can barely move my cock in my pants here, ..."

"Barris, we got a problem."

"*What!* This isn't *enough* for you?"

Hondo swallows. "The backup for the RPG?"

"Yeah? Yeah? *Yeah?*"

"It's out there." He points past the front of the bus.

"Ray, let me get back to you." He squeezes his head around the corner to look where Hondo is pointing and sees the rocket lying about ten yards before them in the rubble.

Just how the fuck did that happen?

Barris drops to his stomach, pointing the rifle out of the cleft where the hub meets the ground, to best tactical advantage, and sets the sights on the Hummer's windshield.

"Hon."

"I know."

"You gotta get that, Hon."

"I know."

"INFIDEL SWINE! YOU HAVE ATTEMPTED TO INTERFERE, WITH MALICIOUS BODILY HARM, A SACRED EVENT! SUCH PROFANITY IS AN AFFRONT TO THE LORD, AND SHALL BE DUALLY PUNISHED! ANY SURVIVORS ARE ORDERED TO SURRENDER YOUR ARMS AND STEP AWAY FROM THE VEHICLE!" The bullhorn squeals as it signs off.

"Fucking hive-mind Centurion drones." Barris switches from full-auto to single shot. The AK-47 bucks hard against his shoulder as he puts one round into the windshield, hearing Hondo take his cue, running behind him. There is a little puff of smoke at the impact point, dead center on the glass, but it barely leaves a scratch.

That new composite is some pretty amazing stuff.

With his next two shots, Barris takes out its front tires...

He hears the shrill whine of the Gatling starting up before clearing the shelter of the bus, and Hondo doesn't even get to sprinting speed when the pavement between him and the rocket sort of erupts, big chunks of the stuff leaping into the air of its own accord. Digging in he reverses direction, back to cover, as the maelstrom follows close on his heels...

Armed figures start to emerge from the patrol cars, and Barris is able to put down two with well-placed shots before the others' return fire drives him to shelter. Over the sound of the small caliber rounds stitching through the bus' skin and ringing off the hub, he hears the soft purr of the Gatling as Hondo rushes by almost horizontal to the ground.

This is not good.

Then the cab above him is melting in a shower of streaking phosphorescence. Back pushed up against the solid steel of the hub, he sees the still-smoldering kiosk before him tear itself apart, and for a small eternity Barris is trapped in the womb of a vortex of violence...

Reaching the shelter of the rear axle, Hondo turns and sees Barris disappear in the carnage of the .50 caliber's onslaught. He pulls out the P-226 and moves to the rear bumper, squeezing off three quick rounds, actually hitting one of the patrol Centurions, before ducking back to cover.

Predictably, the .50 caliber starts tearing its way back through the bus towards him and time stretches as he thinks that maybe today wasn't such a great day to get out of bed, not that he really had a bed, it was more of a futon on the floor of their practice space, but still, it was warm and comfortable with a roof overhead, good people to hang with, preferable to dying out here today; Renee would probably do just fine without him and Barris, after all, she was a drummer, and drummers were always in demand; when all is silent.

A quick glance around confirms that; A] Barris is still alive because, through a parting curtain of debris, he sees him jump up, swinging around the AK-47, and B] The NCA has far too much money and resources to fight intelligently, because in all probability they've just wasted an entire magazine of expensive high-caliber ammo trying to kill two lightly-armed rebels and are currently reloading...

"Barris, the motorcade has stopped a half-click east of your position. You still have a chance of knocking the thing out. Barris? Barris, you still with me?"

Squelching static gives way to a coughing chatter that ends abruptly.

"Ah, yeah Ray, still with you."

"What's your situation? "

"Situation's hot. Ray, but I think we just got a small break."

"Barris, don't be stupid, do it if you can, pull out if you can't."

"Don't think pulling out's really an option here. Ray." More clattering static.

"What's that mean, Barris?"

"Awww, fuck's sake ..."

"Barris? ...Barris, ...*Barris*!"

Barris is cutting loose with the AK-47 on full auto, peppering the Hummer and drawing fire from the patrols, not really doing much damage but at least preventing them from reloading the Gatling, when a familiar shushing sound causes Hondo to turn and see the rocket propelled grenade floating down the street real low and eerie, haloed by its own booster's corona, coming straight toward them and his mind slips to the warm futon near the back of the space, nestled near the bass cabinet, and then the thing's blurry arc scuds overhead, clearing the ruined frame of the bus by no more than three feet, twisting downward slightly to meet with the hood of the Hummer.

The detonation is impressive and intense, spinning the broken Humvee's body to pancake into the underside of the turnpike in a waft of orange flame, the charred and crumpled remains rebounding to the pavement in a cloud of sound and debris.

"Now *dat's* da *shizzle, MUTHAFUCKA!*" Pumping the Kalashnikov, Barris is pointing at him.

Despite his awe at the beauty of the trajectory, Hondo manages to give Barris the finger.

"Well, you sure got it going on in the looks department, but you can't shoot for shit."

Hondo turns at the voice so close it's practically in his ear and he's looking into cool gray eyes sparkling with amusement and mischief.

"Hey, how *the fuck* ..." And then he recognizes her. Squatting next to him, the battered AR-15 slung over her shoulder, he remembers her on stage in some swank Zuppie backer's private underground club, weathered blonde Rickenbaker bass slung in a similar manner, ripping out some righteous backbeat riffs in her R-girl band. Her shaved and tattooed skull has grown out to a cascade of short, bright red waves, her thick lips have at least a couple more rings through them, and the abbreviated Minnie Pearl dress and Doc Marten combo have given way to a funky species of urban fatigues and combat boots, causing Hondo to speculate on the effectiveness of being camouflaged when walking around with a head of bright neon, but the effect on him is pretty much the same.

Astounding.

"Hey, you play bass in 'TWAT'!'"

"Yeah." She smiles, giving him her hand. "I'm Sliver."

"Hondo, ..." He feels the hard calluses on her slender, delicate fingers. " ...I play bass too."

"Who with?"

"Uh, we really don't have a name yet."

Sliver nods.

"You know, you guys' cover of Fugazi's 'KYEO' is really the shit. I can't believe you do double duty on the vocals." He reflexively runs fingers through his muttonchops. "That's a tough riff."

"Nah. That one's easy."

"You play it in drop D?"

"Huh uh. Drop it down to B."

"Wow."

"*Yo,* when you guys are done with your *date,* I could use a little attention here! The Centurions are gonna be pissed!"

Sliver hooks a thumb at Barris. "Who's that?"

"That's Barris." He shrugs. "Singer."

"Oh. Yeah."

"Well he doesn't really sing so much as he grunts and screams, but he's a great guitarist."

"That *is* important."

Hondo can't believe his luck. Seconds ago he was sure he was ready to suffer a horrible, violent, lonely death, and now here he is, with the woman of his dreams actually saving their lives, a goddess and personal icon of his in the local rock circuit. This is a full-on transcendental moment and Hondo is in love.

"Thanks for saving our asses here. That shot was one in a million."

"Zelda popped that one. My sister." She scrunches up her face. "Singer."

"Yeah? Still,..." He's nodding his head and sitting up, trying to assume a more casual stance, getting a better angle on those cool peepers of hers, and she's rising with him, wry smile on her face, and he's hearing his mouth finish the sentence; "...that was full-on edge." Realizing his terrible mistake but powerless to do anything about it...

The remaining two vehicles sprout three Centurions picking around the Hummer's smoldering remains who at once begin to flank their positions, heavy automatic rifles drawn as Barris glances back at Hondo and that strange commando chick he's yammering with. Incredibly, they both stand up.

Just what the fuck do they think they're doing?

When it happens, Hondo is staring at her breast, or rather her right nipple, which, by the topography it projects through the thin fabric of her designer fatigues, is pierced, when three things occur simultaneously:

He hears from behind him Barris shout something

which is cut off immediately by a sharp crack and a large
semi-circular swath of Sliver's chest, the epicenter of
which is the very nipple that Hondo is staring at erupts
with a terrible wet sound. She stands there staring into his
eyes, chasm punched out from her body momentarily
defying gravity, and he sees awareness of impending
death pass in her gaze, when the sheen of Sliver's viscera,
which has splattered over Hondo's face and chest, starts
to run into his eyes. Through the scarlet, viscous haze,
she finally surrenders to gravity, body grotesquely
collapsing on itself in a chromosomal spiral to the
pavement, and the world around Hondo goes gray...

"Barris, talk to me babe."

"Hey, Ray. Yeah, think we're go here in a bit, if Hondo
can keep his cock in his pants."

"Not sure I know what you mean by that, boy-o,
but you better put a rocket in your pocket, 'caus it looks
like a couple of Blackbirds are coming in low, hard and
fast."

"Shit, you serious? "

"They don't look happy, Barris."

"Duly noted Ray." Muted crackling and Barris' voice
off the set; *"Hey, loveb-, .. .ah, God..."* More rustling and

then static.

"Barris, ...Barris? ...*Barris*!"

He leans down to her broken body, the only color in the world, the spark, the minute shard of fading iridescence in Sliver's eyes. Her lips tremble with effort and Hondo touches his cheek to hers to hear, transferring a single tear. Skin hot, dry, her last word leaks with the life from her, inflating a bright bubble of blood.

"Squiggle..."

Hondo's mind reels, the bubble pops, her head lolls lifelessly to the side, and the world snaps back into garish color, over-saturated and unreal. The crimson stain smeared around her open mouth an obscene, gore-flecked lipstick...

Barris watches as Hondo stands up from the fallen chick and starts walking nonchalantly, almost casually towards him. *Stupid mother fucker,* could've been him just as easily as the girl, and here he is, strolling like it's a bright spring day without a care in the world, then he sees that look, the thousand yard stare in his eyes. He knows something's going down.

"Hon, what the fuck you up to?" But he just walks right on past, not hearing, eyes and face blank, slack; he's dragging the rocket launcher behind him, about to step out into the open, practically announcing his presence with the empty metal tube scraping on the ground like that. Then he clears the cover of the bus and there's the flat cracking of the centurions gunfire and the whoop of ricocheting rounds as the ground spits and puffs all around Hondo's feet and Barris just says 'fuck it', checks that he's on full auto, and, leaning out, starts unloading his final banana clip ...

Squiggle.

Why the fuck is that word in his head? Hondo's thoughts are a little jumbled. There are noises around him, kind of like the sound of those mutant South American bees they had so many problems with last year, and he keeps getting peppered with gravel and dirt, so there must be a strong wind he can't really feel. He hears the clattering of Barris' Kalashnikov but it's removed, like a memory. Then there's the rocket lying there, right in front of him. All kinds of stupid, leaving it there like that, and as he's bending to pick it up he discovers the RPG in his hand and it comes in a flash, why he's here, why the rocket's lying in front of him, when something tags him in the left calf hard enough to spin him completely upside down, planting his face in the gravel...

Mentally counting down, just an approximation really, 'caus the AK fires too rapidly to actually count, and it *is* the heat of the battle, Barris is trying to pace himself, keeping his concentration down the sights of the barrel, not looking, not thinking of how Hondo's probably being chewed to pieces by the volley of gunfire he's trying to suppress.

Two patrol cars. Three centurions. And half, correction, *less* than half a clip left.

And, of course, one psycho stupid motherfucking bass player lurching around the field of fire like Superman with a hangover.

The unexpected upside to this is that with Hondo acting as bait, the centurions are going all out wild, giving up their positions, and in quick succession Barris manages to put a round through the helmet of guy #1 from car A, giving credence to an earlier argument with Hondo as to the reasoning behind Barris' preference for armor-piercing ammunition, then he actually hits the rifle of guy #3 from car B, shattering the cheap Government-issue carbine to splinters, rendering him temporarily useless.

The last guy is good. He's got technique *and* Barris

wasting ammo as he ducks and slips shots through his suppression when finally, he makes a fatal mistake, and, dead-on in his sights, Barris squeezes the trigger.

The dry click of the hammer against the empty chamber carries like a sonic boom across the void. Last Guy's head snaps up in sync with his rifle, and Barris is looking down the dark maw of certain death. Though the moment seems to stretch around a mobius-strip of eternity, he barely has time to breathe or even blink before Last Guy's own impotent clack answers him from across the far side of the battlefield.

Another thing those cheap Government-issue carbines do well is jam.

For a wild moment each considers the other incredulously, then Last Guy is frantically clawing at his ordnance and Barris is rifling through the countless chambers of his camo's for the single round he'd pocketed what seems like centuries ago, but in fact was only a few minutes earlier. Front to back, top to bottom he finds his wallet, keys, lighter, a drink ticket dated yesterday wrapped around a severely weathered condom wrapper, small notebook with ballpoint pen stuck in the spiral, sunglasses, cell phone, pot stash, half pack of cigarettes, a small cache of picks, and, ...spare change?

OK. Why does he have so many damn pockets, and how could he commit such a serious breach of combat etiquette as bringing loose change on a mission?

A quick check in on Last Guy and Barris' heart goes black. From the smug expression on his face, the way he snaps the clip home, guesses that the carbine's shortcomings have been trouble-shot, that *he's* just run out of time. Then his fingers find the elusive brass cylinder wedged in the little pocket intended for watches that no one ever uses and again he's looking down the bore of Last Guy's gun when a howling ululation breaks the silence and Barris has time to chamber the round and consider the possibility that Hondo is still alive when the barrel wavers slightly in the direction of the sound.

No time for precision here, so he just goes for the body shot, putting it through Last Guy's bullet-proof vest, seeing his surprise and shock as the carbine ejaculates in his hand, stitching a line of fire across the pavement and up the side of the bar, popping out one of the three remaining windows.

Shit. The Goose is gonna be pissed....

Hondo is beyond pain and way past pissed.

He keeps seeing Sliver and the way her chest exploded, the terror passing in her eyes, and the cocoon of calm around him shatters.

By some freakish trick of the light, bullets are visible scything the air around him in clustered little time-signatures, the faint snapping of their origins syncopating with the noise of Barris' Kalashnikov.

He is screaming as he pushes himself up, a throat tearing, lung searing roar of pure animal rage, expelling gravel and a muddy mucal flow from his mouth, feeling the hot trickle of blood down his leg. Lurching forward, fingers grappling on the ground for the rocket; raising the length of the RPG, sliding it home in the tube against his shoulder; sights up and calibrated, distant awareness of an aural vacuum; lack of sound, bodies on the ground, feeling fusion, connection with the target; knowing with certainty even before the trigger is pulled that the trajectory is true.

The overpass blossoms petals of pulverized pewter heaving the heavy concrete deck-plates upward through whirling clouds of shattered I-beam fragments, the blast pushing him back to the ground with a hot hand, the sound larger even than the last Husker Du concert he'd seen as a kid, decking finally dominoing itself into the valley of the underpass in huge, slow-motion monoliths, pushing out a mushrooming earthbound cumulonimbus cloud of debris, obscuring the carnage and settling over them.

A real-life, real-time fade-out...

"You did it. *Jesus-fuck.* You fuckin' did it."

Goose's ghostly form emerges from the drifting nimbus of flotsam, the bar a dull backlit geometric shape behind him.

Hondo's carrying the remains of Sliver, leaking whatever fluids hadn't already soaked into the ground, reeking because the body had voided itself in death, Barris plodding mechanically next to him shucking empty clips into his pockets, slap of the Blackbirds blades through the air, approaching blindly somewhere through the murk.

"Roll it motherfuckers! In the bar!" Goose's mass is moving with surprising speed towards them, collecting and displacing swirling eddies of ash and soot, hands on the ends of outstretched arms gesturing them to him, and Barris notices the darker streaks leaking out from under his glasses over the gray of his cheeks.

"Hey Goose, .. .you,.. .uh, crying?"

"Nevermind, nevermind,.. .those Blackbirds, .. ."He thuds to a halt when he sees the mess in Hondo's arms. " ...'th fuck?"

Barris shrugs and Hondo just regards him with glazed eyes.

Huge ham hands slap at his face and for a moment it seems like Goose is doing a little bow in front of them, fingers squashing his eyes, jiggling the glasses up on his forehead, voice muffled beneath thick palms.

"Jeez fuck, ..." Then with that amazing ability reserved for gigantic bartenders he is behind them, collaring each in a bouncers cuckold, propelling them both towards the doorway, now surrounded by a shadowy phalanx of regulars. " .. .hearin' that Gatlin', I think,.. .no I *know* you guys are dead. Then when you drop that overpass I think *I'm* fucken' dead, then I see you alive but, .. .but with that poor, .. .*Christ*, you two got me on a fuck of a roller-coaster ri-"

A sound cuts the air around them, a voice slicing time, polytonal contralto as it steps across angelic scales in a winding bel canto, disintegrating with a spiraling arpeggio, that to Hondo's practiced ear is pure beauty, paradoxically considering it is a scream of guttural terror and grief.

Standing before them, ice-blue eyes wide on what's left of Sliver, is the only Caucasian Hondo's ever seen, the RPG tube in her doll-like fingers a startling contrast to the delicate folds of the antique Versace she is wearing, cascading platinum hair and flawless ivory skin casting a luminous halo in the falling ash.

This is Zelda, Sliver's sister…

"Nice job, boy-yo's. Better late that never. The game is FUBAR with all that traffic back-up, and no apparent collateral. *You-know-who* is gonna be pumped. Hey, you getting this? "

Squelch.

"Barris? ...Barris, ...*Barris!*"

Squelch.

"Over-and-fuck-you-out."

THE SIRENS OF FRANKLIN

It was the first time he'd walked up the hill without the stilettos, and its surface felt alien, soft and yielding.

With feet in the flats, his backpack jounced a lot less, and his heels had a shurer purchase, but that wasn't really the point, was it? More unexpectedly, however, was how the slight shift in perspective altered this quotidian experience, the street sloping off at a broader angle, the hill seeming steeper than usual.

It was his chosen time of day, twilight, sun low, raking off rows of houses, billowing trees, passing cars, light; a golden halation. The strawberry daiquiri's left a sweet reek on his palate, drifting pleasantly through the back of his mind as he worked his way up Franklin

Avenue.

A modishly dressed couple approached from the opposite direction, woman regarding him with a disdainful expression, the man rolling eyes as they passed. Without the heels, he attracted far less attention than usual, but more than a few people noticed the budding breasts, Estrogen beginning to flower.

These too, moved around less painfully in the flats, but he missed them, his stilettos. Why he'd abandoned them was lost behind some cloudy scrum generated by his time at happy hour.

The street and foot traffic had reached its crescendo for the day, and he let it wash over and through him, a visual, aural white-noise, that always accessed a lost place deep within.

"Hey *freak!*" A passer-by bellowed, momentarily shocking him to the objective world, but the surrounding clamor, frenetic activity, and harsh planes, pushed him back beneath the surface of his thoughts, that word recalling twisted childhood memories, the abusive violations. Secret humiliation of growing enjoyment.

He took comfort in his attire, the familiar cling of faded ultra-tight Levis, especially around the crotch;

skinny green Polo shirt, gold hoop through left earlobe, and the knitted gray golf cap, pulled snugly over his eyes; beard bristling out from under its brim. Appearance was carefully managed to balance such things, to preserve an order on past, present, and the future, but what of his heels?

His mind traveled back to when he'd first seen them on display, impossibly long, thin, fragile, and they spoke to him with absolute assurance, a promise of a renewed stability, a vibrant and immutable individuality, and from the first time he'd worn them, he believed in their power.

The pained ululation of a siren reached down the Avenue, briefly breaking his reverie, before turning down a side street.

The siren...

The sun had dropped behind the hill, cloaking the Avenue in shadows, and he was vaguely aware of a couple he'd seen before, sitting in lawn chairs before a house that loomed over the sidewalk. The woman was a pretty redhead, the man had dirty blond dreadlocks and tattoos, and they were drinking beer.

"Hey, hillwalker, come up and have a beer." The

woman giggled.

"Yeah, c'mon. It's nice and cold." The man added.

Hillwalker? Who was that?

He continued up the Avenue.

The importance of the familiar. The susurrus of the streaming traffic, drumming manhole covers, the two young men playing guitars on their porch, the guy in the bright orange jumper tending a smoker that chuffed burly semaphores into the still evening air, these occurrences orchestrated themselves about him on this daily jaunt, and their presence assured a stasis few but he realized was so vital.

A passing patrol car let loose an angry war-whoop, dropping into passing gear, big engine stepping up in pitch as it muscled traffic to the shoulder, roof cherries blazing. It disappeared over the crest. Something touched the back of his mind. Thus preoccupied he discovered, almost too late, he'd weaved across the sidewalk, nearly stepping into the street.

Beneath a hand-printed sign that read 'Free Stuff' taped to a street light, clustered at the curb around his feet, was the sad detritus of an uprooted life; faded and broken chair holding an old VHS player next to a ragged

Ren and Stimpy doll, scratched silver boom-box at its feet, nuzzled to a small box of personalized cassette tapes, and a stack of torn paperbacks propping up a calendar that read 'Kittens 1987'. He sensed portent in these talismans.

So many years traipsing this same stretch of Franklin Avenue, Spring, Summer, Fall, and Winter, searching for the perfect balance of object and occurrence, of the earthly and the ethereal, to find the hidden moment in which was locked liberation from the desperate wreckage of the past, that he now, finally, sensed in its approach.

Darkness was feeding on the dusk, turning headlights into luminous torrents of motion, lurching unsteadily down the dimmed sidewalk, he realized the blender drinks had finally kicked in to their full potential, but that too was in the alchemy of the enigma.

The missing heels must be part of the key.

Late, the Mustang fastback, a classic from the sixties, thrummed past, a detonation of noise and luminescence...

Blades of colored radiance sluiced the street, cut through trees, danced off porticos, awnings, serenaded by the bold, trebled voice of the ambulance siren as it pushed up the Avenue in the patrol car's wake, its wail dopplering musically as the vehicle sped by, and there on the sidewalk, he swooned, moved by the beauty of this apparition, noting for the first time in all these years how precisely the architecture of the moment was structured, how intricate all these disparate elements had locked together in a choreographed overture. A hook-and-ladder, slippery with reflections followed closely, pulsing its own plumage into the night.

Breathing rapidly, he attempted to increase his pace, noting how the unaccustomed flats snagged at the cuffs of his jeans, but he pressed doggedly on, topping the rise as the sirens fell to premature silence.

The vehicles had congregated at an intersection, their combined beacons creating a frenetic pool of illumination, halting traffic, attracting a small cluster of people. He hobbled closer.

From the sky, high above, an eye winked open shedding a brilliant xenon tear, bathing the tableau in cool iridescence, angry wallop of the helicopter's blades erupting an omni-directional fugue, trash and grit from the gutters churning to life from the air-wash.

Passing first by the fire truck, then the ambulance, he could see paramedics and patrolmen trying to keep the crowd at bay, but they kept gathering, growing, and moving into the throng; he recognized many.

Holding hands, heads and shoulders slumped, was the mod couple. Just before them, staring transfixed, was the man in the orange jumper, eyes wide, fingers drumming absently at his lower lip. Weaving nearer the edge of the convergence, he passed the two guys from the porch, guitars slung over their backs, engaged in an excited exchange, occasionally craning their necks to see over the people in front of them.

Though the mob became increasingly crowded near the front, he slipped easily between them, unnoticed, and at the leading edge was the couple from the lawn, redhead with the Stimpy doll clutched in one hand, its dead eyes staring up at the night, her face wet with tears, man simply staring ahead, slowly shaking his dreads back and forth, and then he was ahead...

For the barest, briefest of moments he saw a body, broken and torn, splayed and discarded on the asphalt, but that must've been a trick of the light, of the violent cross-winds, because now, before him, looking just as on the day he first noticed them, were the stiletto heeled shoes, arranged as though carefully styled for a photo shoot.

Allured, he hobbled out to them, turning, facing his unseeing audience, their collective gaze fixed on the shoes, faces awash in sweeping chromatic hues, buffeted by swirling gales that held aloft the Avenue's flotsam and jetsam. He grasped the long journey's end, lowering himself slowly to the pavement, discarding the flats, slipping the heels over his feet as the surrounding vehicles loosed a squall of triumph, and rising, embraced by thunder and fire, The Hillwalker joined the sirens of Franklin.

SKYWAY

The hunger has become much more difficult to ignore lately.

In an unconscious act of confirmation, you pull up the jeans bagging around your hips, thinking how well they fit when you bought them brand new last year. When you had your job.

The job that supported your previous existence.

Since that was taken away, life has become a continual succession of countdowns.

Don't.

Thee-hundred twenty-something in checking, two-hundred thirty-five in savings, rent at four-hundred eighty-five in fourteen days, bills round out to about a hundred ...

Stop it.

Twenty-seven in the wallet, thirty-three cents in the pocket, minus three and-a-half for a slice of sausage at Andreas' Pizza, equal to the price of a happy hour beer, unless Billy's working the bar and comps you one; then two beers if you can forgo the pizza. You consult the pack of Camels, cigarettes being a cheap appetite suppressant, if you keep the smoking down. Thirteen left ...

Stop. It.

Of course, there's that check from what's-his-name, the East-Coast guy from that freelance job, two-hundred twenty-five, billed out at net-thirty, but it had been over two months, those funds entering a netherworld of speculative funding ...

Enough.

The mezzanine of Crystal Court teems with office workers released to lunch; people in crisp suits and ties clustered in small enclaves, cubicle brethren, corporate clans, weaving through the sociological stew peopling the Skyway level of the city. They talk amongst themselves, into cell phones, or are internalized by headsets, earphones, ear-buds.

Sucked into the solipsistic void of their hand-held devices, consistently distracted, schizophrenically straddling two worlds, a rapidly escalating infection; smart-phoners. They meander the floor slack-jawed, faces frozen in a rictus of immediate gratification, finger-banging touch-screens of Androids, Iphones, Ipods, Ipads.

This cannot be for the better.

Crash helmeted security guards and city police float silently, eerily between them, perched atop Segways, absurdity of the vehicle's design camouflaged with a vaguely military makeover, presumably to lend it more authority.

Fractured threads of conversations slip over the surface, and you think about their lives, their jobs, their stability that was once yours, and how quickly and completely that has been eliminated.

Just keep moving.

Intercoursing the skyway adjoining the IDS Building to Macys, suspended a story above the street, you witness crystal ziggurats of the city thrusting above into a brittle October sky, a menacing harbinger of the brutal Minneapolis winter to come.

This is no time to go broke.

You used to love winter, growing up on the Mississippi, the frozen body of water infinitely expanding the horizon of your playground, skating over the glassy unbroken plain on the random years that a rogue Alberta Clipper would seize it immobile in black ice. Playing Dog-a-Deer through intricate mazes you and your friends would carve into the covering snow. Tobogganing down every slope and hillock within footfall, building snow-forts; staging epic snowball battles over the chilled, stilled terrain.

So much has changed.

At each café is a queue of people waiting to order, bringing to mind the succulent mix of aromas, renewing wretched pangs of hunger. Crabbed along hallways and clustered around annexes, the restaurants and shops themselves are odd little vestibules of modulated space, most retro-fitted from long-abandoned office suites.

The skyway supports hundreds of these culinary cubbyholes. There are the corporate branches: Starbuck's, McDonalds, Caribou Coffee, Taco Johns, Arbys. Then the more quaintly named individual proprieties; This &

That, Sister's Sludge Coffee, Lite Bite Café, Franks a Million, and the unlikely German Hot Dog & Co. [*special today: walleye fillet sandwich*] Some even creatively boast location within their moniker; Skyway Printing, Skylab, and your personal favorite; The Skywok.

Cloaked in hunger, you push open the annex doors adorned with their ubiquitous 'No Smoking' signs and step onto another gangway swathed in autumnal light, aware that you've abandoned the pizza for the promise of beer. Muted ululations of sirens rise up from the streets below; approaching, departing, overlapping; a consistent testament to the cumulating calamity the world has become.

Do not go there.

Abroad, these constructions are known as skywalks, perhaps a more accurate designation, but you prefer skyway, as it seems to better embrace the concept of this city within a city.

Below, on the plaza surrounding the building's entryway, workmen are busy removing giant granite planking constituting the building's courtyard. Every year these same tiles are disassembled and reassembled for no apparent reason. Like the cyclical and consistent repairs of the system's escalators, these undertakings evidence a vast conspiracy of planned obsolescence.

Down the avenue, you see tiny people moving, as you are, through the tube of an adjacent skyway, and are struck by the disparity of the individual designs; some seemingly formed within wind-tunnels, contours streamlined against supersonic gales. Others are ornamentally bejeweled in stained glass and baroque flourishes, while the bulk of the designers opted for a purely utilitarian approach; vestiges of ancient battleships wrapped in gussets of load-bearing exoskeletons, fusing the facing buildings in an architectonic copulation.

Breaching the far side, you move through the utilitarian passage of the jail building, now charmingly renamed the County Public Safety Facility, yet another example of the current parlance of deception.

Waves of lunchers press through the narrow corridor in opposing directions, a Homo sapien highway reduced to its slowest components: the chronically inattentive, and the grossly overweight. Oblivious rolling roadblocks, bulked up American style, you now see them through third-world eyes; waddling products of a gluttonous, sedentary lifestyle, indifferent to the inconveniences they inflict on their peers, greedily masticating office gossip and comfort foods, bridging them to their next snack or meal.

A barb jabs into your gut, painful, almost rapturous.

So how do you do it? How do you control the hunger?

Well, think of it like this: As a male of the species, it could be argued that sexual appetite is as hardwired to the primal mind as is its nutritive counterpart. Since your longstanding latency in the former territory, it's simply a matter of applying similar negation to the latter.

Christ, are you schizophrenic now, too?

Did you say that out loud?

Just don't think about Her.

But Pandora's box is open, pun intended, and you cringe at the memories.

Of your arrogance and hubris at the apparent trajectory of your success, and of your capacity to take things for granted that should never be. She's not talking to you again…

Stop.

The window displays of the Sky Shoppe are

cluttered with kitsch; small items manufactured in distant lands by child-labored hands, intended to brighten the Xerox days of cubicle culture. The seasonal onslaught of Halloween memorabilia has replaced the fading Fourth of July merchandise. Compulsively collectable Ty plush toys cluster in mock animal phylum beneath corporate motivational posters; the dangling 'hang in there' kitten, and one of a cheetah caught in graceful arc titled 'attitude', somehow ignoring the reality that this beautiful beast is on the brink of extinction. Spinning racks hold greeting cards and patriotic pins emblazoned 'USA' in enameled red, white, and blue. Though only half-full, you cannot recall ever seeing one of these small relics to nationalism adorning a single lapel.

Standing canted against the store's entrance you recognize Lottohead, coin in hand, ritually rubbing at a thick cluster of scratch-cards. Small silver burrs collect in rifts at his feet, tongue-tip darting obsessively in and out his mouth, body rocking back and forth to a personal soundtrack.

Diminutive in stature, he is not quite dwarf or midget, and he has no knees. To ambulate, he uses feet as flippers, legs locked in a lurching robot stride.

Where are his knees?

Clustering the counter, a homogenously attired herd of office Dilberts eagerly hand over cash, biding for their own chance at the latest lottery numbers.

Get rich quick.

The stupidity tax.

That this was such a widespread, accepted addiction amongst the office drone clique was a potentially raw reveal to contemporary human nature. If only people would place the same faith in more pertinent matters, perhaps the world would be a different place.

And who are you to judge?

There are the others:

Jacketman, the elderly African American gentleman, hair and beard turned to wiry white springs, wandering the corridors imploring anyone that would stop to Sharpie their signature on his tattered coat, already opaque with overlapping script, perhaps believing he is collecting wayward souls. You have signed it three times.

Muttering Martha, your basic baglady, sans the shopping cart, favoring battered rolling luggage, upwardly mobile fourteen feet above the street, debating her inner-voice, for all to hear.

Epiphany Earl, [*the Earl of epiphany?*] a younger man; prematurely balding pate threaded with wispy blond hair, grizzled face shot through by clear blue eyes, who will suddenly stop, arms thrust out cruciform, fingers wriggling, mouth working silently, throwing glazed gaze heavenward.

Walkabout, a tall, dark male, patterned tribal scars slashed into his cheeks, skulks the hallways, occasionally breaking quietly into an alien language as you pass. The moniker you've assigned him is intended irony, as he never strays far from the southern reaches of the Skyway's south labyrinth, surrounding the Convention Center.

Chopper, a grizzled man of shifting age, sporting gnarled muttonchops, each ending in a frosty tip, like twin horns, making the rounds toting his own collection of bags. He seems to defy some basic law of physics, becoming thinner, more withered, yet more substantial, each time you encounter him.

And lest we not forget: *her.* A relative newcomer, appearances increasing in frequency; your ex's schizophrenic older sister, seemingly released from her latest County enforced lockdown. Dressed in some personal interpretation of a nun's habit, she claps hands, chanting 'have a nice day', singing it to Stevie Wonder's 'Isn't it Wonderful', the refrain burning into your brain.

Thankfully, she is too lost to acknowledge you're identity.

These are the regulars, and you contemplate whether they are starting to recognize you as one of their own.

Do they have a special name for you as well?

You have become a spectre haunting the relics of your previous life, days twisting and bleeding into one another, washing through to uncountable evenings.

Twinned 'No Smoking' signs separate from the door's motion sensor, and you step out of the mixed hues of fluorescent, tungsten, halogen, and neon into turgid daylight over Fifth Avenue, another leg of your quotidian junket.

A sudden fluting whistle marks the passage of air, pressure between the two buildings attempting to adjust.

On its opposite side is a bustling mezzanine of similar corporate opulence. Another blade of hunger stabs sharply, the countdown unspooling again in your head ...

Stop.

Interesting to note that since they eliminated your job, since you've been spending so much of your time here, you've yet to encounter a single one of your previous co-workers. Perhaps they share your fate.

So why aren't they here?

There are the minstrels, the musicians, drawn here both by controlled climate and superior acoustics. They appear to share a sophisticated system of rotation, for, as you enter the skyway over Third Street, Guitar Guy occupies the area that Blind Accordionist played yesterday, his surprisingly sweet croon resonating pleasantly throughout the interior.

Guitar Guy always has a do-it-yourself display set up on the ventilator nearby. A hand-lettered sign proudly boasting '25 years in the skyway' sits next to a careful arrangement of music CD's beneath a battered case crammed with curios; an array of hard-candies, the omnipresent Ty plush toys, and, of course, hard currency; his earnings for the day. His repertoire of classical acoustic tunes is competent; however, upon closer examination, the lyrics have been subtlety altered to accommodate a decidedly leftist political agenda.

Blind Accordionist is just that, an elderly man shielded by dark glasses mutely working the bellows and keyboard, his oeuvre recalling blazing fall foliage on crisp Oktoberfest days.

More of a seasonal offering, the Jesus Singers appearances increase as Christmas approaches. Whether theirs is an homage or satire of the bawdry black minstrel arias of old is open to debate, but their sincerity is not. The troupe consists of two men separated by at least a generation, possibly father and son, rhythmically stamping feet and slapping thighs, belting out the Word Of The Lord, wishing passers by to 'have a great day', insisting that 'Jesus loves you'.

This is just a sampling. There are others, many others.

Years ago a young woman frequented these corridors, clad festively in a flower-print dress, knee-length black and red striped stockings capped by Doc Marten boots, playing dreadfully incompetent banjo. She always had a warm smile for you.

You wonder what happened to her.

Braving the pedestrian currents, small caravans of

cherubic toddlers sit cooing, screaming, gurgling, and drooling, within plasticized multi-seated Playschool trains, pulled along by fresh, pink-faced *au pairs*; the parent corporation's child-care policies in action.

There are the miniature, single-seated golf-carts; Rascal's, for those that have simply grown too large or slothful to move about under their own volition; reverse bionic people, technology reinforcing their deficiencies.

And legion are the wheelchairs in this zone of Draconian handicap construction regulations, where they thrive and even seem to multiply; diminutive posse's of whirring homunculi aggressively thrusting themselves through the ambulatory, perhaps in retaliation for nature's cruel Darwinism.

A cowcatcher would be a fitting accessory.

Power-walkers pass in clusters of two's and three's; She-Dilberts trading dress shoes for sneakers, out on a hearty workout over their lunch hour, wheezing noisily, trading breathy bursts of rumor and innuendo. Only within this society, at this point in history, could mere walking be considered exercise.

Flocks of blind, some leading seeing-eye dogs, navigate the crowded walkways, antennae-tapping orange and white canes, tripping up distracted smart-phone drones.

Intimate covens of pregnant women navigate the crowd, fingers maternally stroking tumescent tummies.

Breed lusters.

Their numbers exploded exponentially, the uncreative filling a void with procreation. A long-term investment in denial of a deranged and poisoned planet, ironically brought about through unchecked overpopulation.

And the beggars; everywhere the beggars and the homeless; a sure sign o' the times, brother. Hungry eyes, mumbling mouths, and needy, greedy, outstretched hand-lettered signs inciting an unfamiliar outrage, causing you to consider the rift in humanity that separates the giver from the taker. *You* have never taken welfare, collected food-stamps, filed for unemployment, or asked for hand-outs.

Even now.

It is also interesting to note how the sudden increase in the presence of the homeless has brought about an utter disappearance of public restroom access; even the water fountains have vanished or been shut down.

The klaxon of a security scanner breaks into your thoughts. Originally, your reaction would be a guilty hesitation, an anticipation of interference from security, but now it just registers as another aural aggravation. Long ago you realized that these devices were set to go off at random.

Fear as control; a microcosm of the world's political climate.

There is a certain flow, an unspoken etiquette here, noticeable only when broken: as pet peeves targeting impediments to your transit scroll through your mind; the dawdlers, the halt-and-spin, the left-lane blind-corner-cutters; you add another to the list.

The drafters.

Smart-phone drones who will stand idle, enraptured with product in hand, making a sudden distracted decision dropping into step behind you, well inside personal space, still transfixed by their screens.

Sudden stops are a temporary cure.

You luck into a free food sample before 'Sushi-on-Skyway', but the rich flavors of raw tuna, rice, and wasabi from the thin morsel of California Roll merely aggravate your appetite.

As a distraction, possibly, your mind wanders to the time you nearly stepped on the wet dollop of a turd lying plainly on the floor, its presence unacknowledged by the crowd, but for a teeming rift in the traffic pattern.

Its presence still troubles you.

You enter the skyway above the County Courthouse's Courtyard, currently occupied by the local chapter of Occupy Wall Street. A cluster of business-suited professionals lean over the balustrade scrutinizing the group below, mocking the gathering; gutterpunks mostly, dragging crude signs and banners, a ragged group barely numbering a dozen; a pathetic representation of the supposed ninety-nine percent

Surrounding them is a phalanx, double their number, of armed officers and deputy sheriffs, radiating dark authority. Their protective presence there, accorded an outraged media, was drawing hideous amounts of overtime from the dangerously unbalanced State Budget, all to ensure that that the protesters comply with newly minted laws restricting their behavior.

It's all become such a terrible joke.

Not that you don't sympathize with them. Indeed,

considering your current circumstances, you couldn't agree more with their grievances. It's just that you can only find futility in their actions. Because the system has always been fixed, the cards already stacked against the majority, by the few financial elite, embedded so deeply within its fabric, for so long, and driven by such unrestricted avarice, that they would never willingly surrender what they control.

Not without force.

Not without blood.

You press on.

Thing is, the real true blue thing of it is, you've never operated by plan, never had a real outline, no far-reaching structure to your life. No 'where do you see yourself in five years'.

Your modus operandi was always instinctual, by rote, sensing the most immediate opportunity to carry through to the next, the most available future.

And there was always one there; you knew it, could perceive it, a direction to guide you. And it worked. It worked for so long you took it for granted, Big Irony here.

Because now it is gone.

When you reach out, there is only void. An absence. Naught. The countdown running through your head is real. Final.

And this is a soul chilling truth.

And what are your options, really? To become one of these lost, wandering refugees? To be constantly craving food, warmth, rest. Unwashed, filthy; constantly scurrying out from under the ire of one security guard, or similar authoritative figure, just to be displaced by another?

This is not an option.

And not for the first time, you consider It, whether you will have the courage, once the time comes, to go through with It, when the countdown reaches zero. The jump, the gun, the pills, the blade; you know you lack the conviction to do such a thing in the end.

You simply have no future.

Stop.

The system leads through an open parking ramp to its outer reaches. You are seized by alien dread turning a familiar corner. One of the storefronts stands darkened, windows draped with makeshift veils, and a notice is posted behind the glass door:

Notice to customers of

RB Jewelers

The owner of RB Jewelers passed away unexpectedly

on August 30.

Until further order of the appropriate court this

business is closed.

Notification and information regarding the claim
process for return of property will be posted as
soon as it is available.

We apologize for any convenience.'

You remember a humble giant of a man stationed behind the counter, greeting customers with a soft Slavic accent, delicately demonstrating the internal workings of clocks and watches with his oversized digits. You see timepieces adorning the darkened walls still holding time, pendulum's marking rhythm, knowing they will all stop without his presence, and you are seized by a sudden and complete grief at the silent negation of this gentle soul.

Harbingers everywhere.

Time twists, and you are someplace else.

A kiosk displays a glowing Duratrans of the city grid, super-imposed by the branching mandala of the skyway system threading throughout it. Something on the map catches your attention; an arm that reaches far north.

Unexplored territory.

Consulting the legend, you find that *You Are Here*, and set off for the unknown, a persistent niggling of foreshadowing scratching the back of your mind.

The directions lead past a Chipotle chain choked with patrons corralled between portable partitions, spilling into the hallway, down a deserted corridor that snakes through the bowels of the building. Mottled beige walls and dropped acoustic ceiling claustrophobically close in around you. Hushed noises of ventilation suggest arrhythmic respiration.

There are no shops or offices here, just anonymous unmarked doors and fungal, old building smells. The passage takes unlikely serpentine turns and switchbacks, and by the time you notice the ensuing silence, you realize you are alone.

With the layoff, all other elements of your life started dropping away, as if sensing some infectious malignancy, and you understand why the others come here. Faced with utter solitude, it is an innate desire for companionship, a final attempt at forging a bond with humanity.

Dead end. Wrong turn.

Confused, you backtrack; find a single 'No Smoking' door leading through a mini-skyway straddling an alley, juncturing another passage. Equally deserted and indistinctive, this is tinted in a tasteless marine green by ancient, stuttering fluorescent fixtures above cubed chromium grating within the ceiling. Turning a corner, you hesitate before the next annex.

From across an unknown street is an unfamiliar building, constructed in the New Brutalism style of the sixties, its harsh concrete planes veneered in pebble wall masonry. The skyway itself appears to have been added as an afterthought, cantilevering at an angle to bond with the structure's side. Narrow, the gussets outside are bubbled and scarred with rust, floor slanted downward, the faded, patterned carpet worn threadbare, covered with a mosaic of ancient stains.

Standing at its opposite side, sentinel, is a solitary figure. At your approach, Epiphany Earl's deep cerulean eyes find and hold you, and he speaks clearly.

"The beginning is the end."

A nod, and he shuffles off the way you came. You face doors that for some reason don't seem right, naked, and it takes a moment to register the absence of 'No Smoking' signs.

The foreshadowing turns malevolent, merging with the hunger. Bowels cramping, you try not to swoon. You find yourself in a vaulted atrium of scalloped chromium ribbing, delicate dangling fixtures; a gleaming Logan's

Run version of the future, all somehow terrifyingly familiar. The shops here have the appearances of the vernacular; forced and formed from their office origins, the designs quaintly old-fashioned, though evidence strongly suggests that these are recent constructions.

All of which registers only peripherally, as your attention is immediately wrested to the room's inhabitants.

It is populated with chimeral apparitions ...ghosts.

You attempt to stagger from the paths of these gossamer wraiths, flowing fluid skeins of insubstantiality, ebbing and drifting throughout the lobby, deliquescing the air, leaving whispered phantom echo's.

The floor goes liquid beneath your feet, the incorporeal reflecting swirling patterns throughout the polished soffit. Turning in disbelief, you find yourself facing the darkened, chained entry of an abandoned cubby; single fixture illuminating a space tiled in a cheery seventies motif. Something about the pattern resounds in your mind.

Leaning on the wall, trailing down the hall, you come up against a plaque, a map; one charting a very different system.

It is from a previous time. Architectural, quaintly nostalgic, it's an illustration depicting a far simpler city. An archaic hieroglyph of runnels that interconnect a few of the city's central structures, terminating at a very unlikely point.

Powers Department Store.

This cannot be.

It's a mistake. A joke.

Historical marker?

Powers was shut down in the mid eighties. Torn down in ninety-two.

You were there.

You've seen it countless times from outside, the truncated phallus of the old skyway looming over the parking lot where the building once stood, yet after a few confirmative turns down the hallway, you face the impossible through glass doors before the final threshold.

It stands shimmering, a radiance of portent, a reification, a memory new again. The massive façade is furled in colorful striped awnings, distinctive cursive logo scribed against the brickwork, but something in the perspective is skewed, dizzying; for, even as the building stands directly across the street, the interconnecting skyway seems to run on farther, to lead through, beyond, and you hesitate as déjà vu builds to a tsunami within your mind.

Go.

Entering the corridor, it is an olfactory time capsule, smells of recent industrial carpeting commingling with cloying patchouli, over the permeating reek of stale tobacco, and there are spectres here of an altogether different nature ...

A blissfully entwined couple passes, man in beige, tight-fitting bell-bottoms, glossy brown loafers, and a deep-knit, bright-red turtleneck sweater, sporting a Sonny Bono mustache, bushy sideburns, and the sprayed, sculpted, layered hairstyle that was known as 'The Drylook'. (*The wet-head is dead*)

The woman's belted gingham pantsuit is garishly multicolored and dated, as is her Farrah-feathered blond hair and oversize oval sunglasses.

The familiarity is frightening, the dappling sunlight seeming *newer, cleaner.*

Freshly painted walls scroll past as two boys scamper by, the younger in brown corduroy's, golden locks spilling over horizontal rainbow stripes of his tee-shirt, followed by a friend in elephant-bottomed jeans you wore as a child. He's got on a pastel green button-up shirt, oversize collar snapped straight, mop of brown hair cut Bobby Brady style. Mom gives pursuit, pink leggings scissoring beneath a bright flower-printed dress, hair *very* Mary Tyler Moore, and your legs have lost their feeling.

Somehow the skyway's terminus keeps sliding closer, as two men in ridiculously checkered leisure suits over-take you, smelling of a three martini lunch, one actually *smoking a cigarette*. The sudden, forgotten taste of chocolate malt is in your mouth, the song 'Summer Breeze' faintly audible, a haunting leitmotif, and the portico to Powers is before you. The glass doors beyond the old sales floor open up and out, supported by vaulting colonnades, proffering yesterday's products, and it comes back…

A brisk, clear October day, smoky smell of hickory, the flush potential of Halloween, Christmas to come, and the warmth of your parent's house, comfort of their enduring proximity. The eager anticipation of a trip to the big city, a visit to the department store, a place of dreams, offering enchanting, magical objects, your future a promise, an unseen spark on an infinite horizon, and *here* is where you belong, within this memory, the only future that remains…

The past.

You open the doors.

Addendum:

[AP] Minneapolis, MN - A violent explosion that destroyed an abandoned skyway in downtown Minneapolis during rush hour yesterday remains a mystery.

At approximately 5:04 PM, the blast ripped through the heart of the city, shattering windows for blocks.

"It's a miracle no one else was killed or injured." Commented Police Chief Rhybys, during a press conference last night, referring to the fact that Marquette Street, directly beneath the incident, was closed due to construction.

"At this point in the investigation we can't go into details, but we believe there is no further threat to the public. The bomber was the only casualty. We are still seeking to identify the suspect, and are pursuing all missing persons leads available."

The skyway formerly connected Fifth Street Towers to the Powers Department Store Building, which was torn down in 1992, and subsequently sealed off from the public. It is unclear how the bomber gained access.

Rhybys, when queried about the possibility of domestic terrorism, responded:

"While all occurrences of this nature are investigated by the FBI as possible acts of terrorism, I have personal doubts about this particular event. It was not a target of opportunity, the timing had no significance, and there are no apparent victims besides the alleged bomber himself.

It simply makes no sense."

GIG

That fucking smell.

It hits him the instant he passes through the backstage door, taste of coming home from the road. A sweet-sour mélange of stale alcohol, staler vomit, holding a distinct background tone of body odor and urine, spiced slightly by hints of illicit smoked substances.

"Gae a move on, Hundoo, ya fookin tube!" Frenchie barks. Hondo realizes he'd been in one of his trances.

Frenchie, Stage Manager, was in fact not French. He was Scottish, and his Edinburgh accent sounded suspiciously like all the characters in that old movie, 'Trainspotting'.

A guitar case slaps Hondo's back, Barris shoving past, leather jacket creaking from the cold. "Wakey wakey, Hon. Get your gig on."

An articulate series of taps ride his spine, stalling annoyingly on his neck. Renee slides by, rolling her drumsticks down his jacket's zipper, chiming off the tab. She smiles, flips the sticks, grabs him by the muttonchops, pushing mouth and tongue to his.

He digs into the kiss. Stepping back, Hondo considers her form bundled against the winter, knowing too well the toned figure that lurks within. Her eyes burn.

"You ready for this, Hon?"

"If I wasn't feelin' the love before, Ray? Feelin' it now."

Her smile broadens as she yanks the aviator cap from her head, releasing a messy black bob. "Good to see you back, babe. Will we rock tonight?"

Hondo has to return that smile. "Righteously."

He follows his band-mates, snaking through narrow corridors stacked to the ceiling with cornucopia of music and mixing gear, through milling throngs of performers, roadies, and technical worker slaves, maneuvering his bass case through the spaces.

Standing sentinel at the doorway of the greenroom, the room actually painted an alarming blood red, was Goose.

"Barris...Renee...Hondo. So pleased you could grace us with your divine presence."

The club's manager, booking agent, and spiritual epicenter looms above the three, ushering them into the room. Barris smacks him in the shoulder. "Hugs and kisses to you too, Goose."

"It's been awhile. You're late. One develops certain concerns."

"You know you love us." Renee taps a tetrameter up the jamb, following Barris inside.

"Where the problem lies." He stares down at Hondo, benevolence of his gaze magnified through lenses of the old-timey things before his eyes. Glasses. "You good for this, Hon?"

"No worries, G. Missed this shit, yo? Just glad to be back." They exchange an intricate handshake. Hondo points. "Though, it should be noted, your concern is quite heartwarming."

Goose grunts, scowl crossing his face. "Just doin' my job. Running the show." He reaches into a down vest, producing a stack of printed stubs. "Drink tickets; food tickets. Get yourself a bite to eat. You're looking a little dwindled."

"Sweet." He holds them up for the others to see.

Barris hooks a look over his shoulder. "Rider, Goose? We got a rider?"

Goose sighs. "That would be the cooler with you guy's name on?"

"Jag? You remember the Jag?"

"What you think, Hon?"

"Double sweetness. You the man, G."

"Sound checks at six. You're on at midnight. Prefer you headline, but know you guys like runner-up, so you're opening for 'Correxit'. Welcome back."

"Shit, Goose…" Two heavily bearded roadies push past bearing travel cases. Hondo marshals Goose back out into the hall. "About our last gig here; I was…I…"

Goose stops Hondo with a hand. "You saw a beautiful thing die badly. That kind of thing tends to fuck people up."

"Yeah? Barris was there. He didn't crack."

"Barris is a danger-bait, psychopath, stage ninja. The man excels, but he's dead cold inside. You got heart,

Hondo. Stay that way."

"I got heart?"

Rolling eyes, Goose blasts out a sigh. "Never fucking mind. I got a club to babysit. Talk to Frenchie about help with your gear." He slips away through the hall's melee with typically unusual grace for a person of his physical stature.

The greenroom beckons.

Hondo moves into the space, it's familiarity a welcoming comfort.

Inside are all the usual suspects.

Giff, Tiff, and J-peg from 'Deselect' are brazenly sharing a joint with Pay-lo, bassist for 'Weak Tornadoes' in the west corner. Pay-lo's head being shaved, haloed by a fiery red, right-angled Mohawk. Barris talking smack about 'The Arsonists' with Lydia and Gaff of 'Shape-charge.' Members of the Dub-Step group 'Boiling Nails' had encircled Renee, rapping beats as she playfully shed layers of winter clothing.

"Godfuck, if it ain't the man himself. We all heard you went section eight." Wynkyn stands next to Hondo. Drummer of 'Correxit', he was a small, hard man of tight words and movements, beneath a towering pompadour.

Also just happened to be a member of the commando rebellion cell that Hondo had been part.

Hondo's smile was sad. "Yeah, Wynk, I lost it. Everyone fucking knows."

"So you're back."

"Yeah."

"You just back, or you back-back."

"Just the music."

Wynkyn glares, muscles shifting beneath tattoo sleeves.

Hondo shucks his shoulders. "For now."

Wynkin half-grins as band-mates Blynkin and Nod approach. He dips the pompadour at Hondo.

"You just better rape that stage tonight. Music's the end-all, yeah? But we need vets out there. Losin' some good people. Toe-cutter? You heard?"

"I heard."

"Bad guys are winnin'."

"I heard."

"Hon! Shit! Hon, man! Shit! Motherfucker! Whoa! Hon!" Blynkin is amped up on something, nearly checking Hondo's face with the headstock of his Gibson leaning in to shake his hand, jerking it like an electrocution.

"Blynk. What the fuck?"

"Fucking. Shit, you know?"

"Yeah, Shit fucking."

"Motherfucker! Knowhatimsaying?"

Nod stumbles through his mates, eyes heavy. He slowly embraces Hondo.

"Return of the prodigal son."

"Yeah. Biblical."

Backing off, Nod offers a stoned smile. "That it is."

Hondo felt good.

It had been awhile.

*   *   *

That one. Bet he's fucking hung.

Renee mentally checks herself. This was getting out of hand. The prospect of the oncoming gig had whipped her libido super-cell, and here she was, back to the bar, staring at dude's crotches. Pathetic. She tips back a Jag shot, chasing it with a PBR tallboy.

But fuck it, right? This is what it was, what she did, what she loved, and those feelings were just some kind of toxic cultural atavism held over from the Fundamentalists. Sex had always been part of the music. Kinda' the point, really.

The place was beginning to fill, and she scans the room to locate her crew, trying to remember when she'd last screwed them.

Not together. No, Barris and Hondo each held to some anachronistic macho sensibility that drew a line at crossing the sexes, but that was OK. They each had their merits.

Not tonight though. Not either of them. The situation was fucking fragile. Nearly a year since Hondo had his very public meltdown and disappearance.

Over a chick.

Well, Sliver did die violently before his eyes. That would be bad, especially considering she was a fellow bass-player, one of his idols. And the firefight had been fucking harsh.

But the cost was too high. Them being a band, them being a group, a field unit, Dante, architect of the revolution, ordered their cell to sleep, at a time the Fundamentalists were inflicting very heavy losses. Word being it was now all-out Civil War.

And not just them. After she bit it, Dante shut down 'TWAT', Sliver's band as well. Zelda, her sister, singer in the band, had gone Fukushima over the dual loss.

All that idle time and talent, wasted.

Then Hondo, appearing at her crash last month, all dreamy-eyed, remorseful, talking of the band, the music, just the music. Hondo of the intense, thorough fuck.

Renee checks herself again.

Goddammit. This is what it must be like to be a dude.

Shaking her head, she spies Barris talking up a groupie type back by the wings. Obvious, by the girl's body language and attire. Or lack thereof. Fluttering eyes, machine-gun laughter, pouting lips, wetted frequently by a raptor tongue. Barris, totally on the make.

Girl better be ready for the swinging death in his pants. Freakishly huge, really. Equal amounts pleasure and pain.

That's fucking it!

Renee grabs the tallboy off the counter, heads backstage. Has to warm up. Has to change her look. Something in the air tonight. She needs to be ready for anything.

*   *   *

Fucking Bambi?

"Your name is Bambi."

"Yah."

Barris considers the creature before him: pretty first-class groupie material. An Object if there ever was, shoulders rolling, hips pulsing, fingers kneading her ass. And that tongue. Definite possibilities here.

"That first or last?"

"First, last is Bumper."

"Bambi Bumper."

"Pretty much." She smiles with her body. "I, like, know all about you guys."

"What you mean?"

"Got your whole collection on Radcast."

"We've… never recorded."

"Someone did. That song, 'Spitless Eyeholes'. Is. The. Fuck." That tongue again. "I mean I really actually like to fuck to it."

"Radcast got 'Spitless Eyeholes'?"

"Yah. Bunch more too."

"No fuck."

"Yah."

Barris leans close, drinking in her lust. "You know,... Bambi, ...Thumper, whatever...this poses an interesting quandary, kinda' unique to artists such as myself. While I definitely want, no, check that, *need* to fuck, the last thing I wanna' hear while doing shameful things to you, is my fucking band."

"Really?" Look of general confusion. "Most singers get off on it."

"I'm not *most singers*."

"I've heard." She pulses against him. Barris grabs a handful of Bambi's ass, grinding their crotches together. Her eyes go big. He spots Frenchie towing Hondo through the growing rabble over her shoulder; backs off, addresses her cleavage.

"Gotta' set the gig up. Sound-check and all that. Come backstage about two hours. Warm me up. You're familiar with its location?"

"Chi-yah." Bambi blows away a dangling curl from the side of her head that isn't shaved.

"Bahrriss…" Frenchie's over-rolling the R's,

displacing current tenements in the vicinity, Hondo dogging him.

"Frenchie. You know Bambi, here?"

"Aye, ah ken the wee lass. Howzit then, Bahmbi?"

"Super, Frenchie. " Her eyes jump over his shoulder. "Hey, is that Hondo?"

"Whoa, girl." Barris frames her face with his hands, turning her back to him. "Why court the help when you've already got the royalty's attention?"

Eyes rolling, Hondo throws him the bird.

Barris turns to Frenchie. "Bambi's with me tonight, French-man. She gets in the Green Room."

"Nae Problem." Frenchie scratches at a pointed, graying goatee, nodding a chin to the bar. "Goat the Marshal combo oapstage oan moic'd. Sting-Ray's tuned the Strat, the SG, ahnd thot fookin weird Travis Bean thingy you've goat." Eyebrows knotting beneath a balding pate, he hooks a thumb over shoulder. "Canna' believe your man here's still playin' thot shitey Gretsch."

Hondo leans in. "Hey, yo? That's my piece you talkin' about." He shrugs. "'Sides, it's all I got."

"Aht least change the fookin' strings."

"Empty there."

"Sting-Ray's bound ta have a set aroond."

"For a short-scale?"

Bambi's attention goes to the ceiling. "So,... yah. I'll leave you boys to your band thing." About-facing, she twists back to Barris. "Later."

"You know it."

The three pause a beat to consider her retreating form.

"Barry fanny, that."

"Damn straight."

Hondo slides into Bambi's space. "So Frenchie, like, to you, fanny means..."

"Aye, whoat yea Americans so crassly refer to as; pussy."

Barris grabs a bottle precariously perched atop a rotten run of wainscoting. "Don't know, Frenchie. Fanny sounds pretty crass too."

"Yea Yanks doont' grasp the subtleties oaf the King's fookin' English."

Hondo laughs. "Seriously, French? The way you Hibernians throw around the word cunt?"

Frenchie's eyes go wide. "But it's never to women like, ya radge! It's a terhm of endearment."

"Right. Maybe where you come from, …" Hondo gives him a sly smile. "…wherever that is."

Frenchie's eyes narrow. "Ah doont' lahke the soond' oaf that."

Barris slaps his back. "Goddamn Frenchie, we've missed you! Defo no love lost."

"Spunkbubbles!" Frenchie pushes off into the crowd, pointing backward. "The lot oaf yea!"

He disappears.

Barris settles into the wall. "Frenchie's the ace of stage."

"True dat." Hondo scratches his back on an outcropping of trim, turning to the room. "Ah, Christ."

Following his gaze, Barris eyes the couple in a booth against the far wall, hands clasped, heads bowed, lips moving, eyes downcast, basket of some deep-fried food composite between them. Barris bristles.

"Just what. The fuck."

*   *   *

Fuck!

Barris moves past Hondo, Hondo grabbing his

arm. "Barris? *Barris*!" Spins him. "Not here, yo? Club's neutral."

"Just gonna' talk." He turns and breaks ice through the crowd.

"No you're not." Hondo follows.

The couple's ensemble severely contrasts the club's surrounding style. From a different time. The woman's hair in finger-curls. Face: blush and lipstick. Cashmere sweater, turquoise poodle skirt, bobbysocks. He an off-white button-down beneath brown blazer, clean-shaven, flattop buzz cut. The khakis seemed out-of-place. The spit-shined penny loafers do not.

Their reverie is spoiled by Barris' approach.

"Hey, are you ...*praying*?"

She looks up slowly, reproachfully. "*Yes*. Yes we are." That morally elevated light in her eyes.

The man breaks his hand-temple, grasping her around the wrist, head still bowed. "Karen..."

"Well then..." Barris steps up to her corner of the booth. In practiced motions he pops his buckle, buttons down the fly of his jeans, pulls free a heavily endowed semi-erect member. "...guess you won't mind this."

Karen's eyes boggle as he starts hammering the

thing's circumcised crown off the table, clattering the dishes.

The man looks up, a tortured expression shaping his face. "Please…"

"Ho! Shit. Yo, Barris?" Hondo dances up from behind, pulling his friend back, stammering to them. "Sorry! You know…sorry." Despite his shock, Hondo can't stop giggling. "My friend here…you know, gets a little…"

Karen sneers at their retreat. "Heathenous *pigs*. You will burn in eternal *hell*." Attention never straying from his cock.

"See?' With Hondo dragging him back, Barris redoubles his masturbatory efforts. "Don't like when *I* do it, huh? Oh, wait!" He points at Karen. "You do! *That's* the problem! You *do*!"

The couple gets lost in traffic. "Turn it the fuck down, Barris." Hondo still giggling, hauls him toward backstage. "And hey, yo? Put that thing back in your jeans."

"You saw it! What they were doing? Deliberate *provocation*!" Barris' tone indignant.

Still struggling, Hondo skirts a crowded table. "And

it worked. Didn't it?"

Barris thrashes about, facing him, and Hondo has to parry to avoid being dick-wacked. "They are the fucking enemy, Hondo!" He chin-jabs back to the club. "They're the ones who've been raping our minds and killing our people! *Every! Fucking! Day!*"

"Could you scream that a little louder?" Renee, birthed by the crowd, appears, naked, but for a delicate spider-webbing of fabric that gathers just enough at her mons pubis and breasts to be just shy of transparent, black studded collar, and a pair of bad-ass combat boots. Her muscles gleam and ripple when she seizes Barris' neck and slams him into the wall. "I don't think the folks at the back of the bar quite heard that."

"Whoa, Renee." He chokes out.

Hondo's eyes are agog. "Yow, yo? You hotter than love."

"Listen *fuckwads*." Her fury upticking. " Keep your fucking voices down, and your opinions to yourself. We *cannot* afford to be exposed. I don't want to have to report this to Dante." Releasing Barris, glancing down, a peculiar mix of disgust and lust crosses her face. "And put that fucking thing back in your pants."

"Yes ma'am." Barris gives her a little mock salute.

Hondo can't keep his eyes off her. "Sorry Ray. Just that we caught this couple praying up front…"

"Praying? *Here?*"

"Yeah. I know, right?"

"Shit." She absently runs fingers over abs, and Hondo so wants to put his tongue right there. "Still," regarding them both deeply. "…this is our night. Nothing stops us. Nothing gets in our way. Tonight, *we* are fucking God."

"Righteous."

Barris is nodding. "Amen, sister."

"Good." Abruptly she about-faces. In the beat before she disappears through the throng, Hondo gets a perfect glimpse of her perfect ass in perfect motion.

Fuck.

*   *   *

Now look what the fuck you got me doing for you, Sliver.

Zelda struggles against the dead weight of the bass case through once familiar corridors, sensing the disembodied presence of her sister, to the closed door of the greenroom.

Guarding it is Frenchie, whose expression, when he spots her, shifts from shock to delight. "Aye, this night. Loike fookin ghosts driftin' the bahkstage," He crosses beefy arms. "Grand ta see ya, Zelds."

He seems sincere, and she's kind of touched. "Been a bit, yeah?"

"Thot it has. Howzit then?"

"Fucked up, Frenchie. Tonight though?" She holds up the case. "Got a debt I need to collect."

Nodding, he opens the door. "Say nae more."

She drifts in and it's like a time machine. The crimson walls henpecked by countless strata of graffito and band tags. Cumulous clouds of things being smoked drifting between pockets of people talking, drinking, laughing, plinking and tuning instruments, all vibing a nervous anticipatory intensity. The colors, smells, sounds, draw something up from deep inside, an emotional battering-ram that threatens to burst forth, tear her to shreds, but she spots *them*, more or less together, near the back, by the bathroom. Setting the case before her, she makes a B-line in their direction, ignoring all the heads suddenly turned to look.

Hondo is slouched in the corner, worse-for-the-wear short-scale bass hung from gaunt shoulders, bottle of jaggermiester cocked off a hip, trademark muttonchops drifting to premature grey, talking to a small dude beneath a huge pompadour.

Renee is naked. No, check that, she's got on some mean looking boots and is kind of covered in thread-like filaments that throw a living pattern over a killer toned and very exposed body. She's tapping a complex meter on the bathroom door, probably pissing off the person trying to get business done inside.

Barris is…well Barris is getting a blow-job. Leaning back against the wall, eyes heavenward, hips slowly pulsing a rhythm, trying push a few more inches of monster cock into the mouth of the chick with the half-shaved head that is kneeling before him, Zelda is reminded of a documentary she's seen at some point in her life of a snake that could unhinge it's jaw to eat rabbit whole. Must have some serious gag-reflex control.

She stops before them, and Hondo, who's taking a drag from the bottle, sees her and spits out the mouthful into the little dude's hair sculpture.

"Zelda?" He gasps.

The other two turn their sights on her, and the girl on her knees mumbles something indistinguishable.

Zelda points the bass case. "Didn't your mama tell you never talk with your mouth full?"

*   *   *

Zelda? White-witch from 'TWAT'? The fuck is this?

Renee is in an altered state. The Caucasian complexion of the chick is throwing haloes around the room; skin a creepy translucency that actually reveals veins in her face. Hair so white it actually looks silver. Tiny thing too, clad in an ashen, petite, lacey, number, dwarfed by the leaden gig-bag by her side.

White on silver on porcelain on white.

Zelda strikes attention from Barris' knob-job to Hondo and lobs the case into his arms. "Open it."

Still wearing a shocked look, Hondo slowly, carefully works the zipper, like he already flashes its contents, freeing an elegantly classic Rickenbacker 4003 bass, bearing a patina that only comes with loving care and years on the road. Fingers moving reverently along the strings, the curves of its body, his eyes grow wide. He looks to Zelda. "I don't understand."

"Was Sliver's." She shakes out her carrying hand. "No use to me now. Want you to have it."

"Me...?"

"'Cause, you know...you were there when..."

"But..."

"One little caveat." She crosses alabaster arms webbed in blue veins. "I play with you tonight."

Whoa. Renee, for once, is too dumbstruck to formulate a response.

"Wait! What? Ah, ahh...ooh...*ahhh.*" Barris' hips bronco, Bambi hanging on for dear life, throat pulsing with the effort of trying to swallow.

Zelda turns chin up and away from the spectacle, trying to preserve a little dignity. "Can't these two at least use the bathroom?"

Renee taps a triplicate on said door. "Been locked for the last hour at least. Startin' to think maybe an OD?"

Gretsch forgotten against the back wall, Hondo walks up to Zelda cradling the Rickenbacker. " I think it's a great idea."

"Hold on!" Barris is buttoning back up, stepping around Bambi. "No way. No fucking way! Us three are the band."

"Wait just a fuck!" Renee pumps a fist, Barris actually flinching back, stopping. "Think about it."

"Think about what? We are a power trio. Classic structure. Magic number. Occurs in nature."

"Like what, Barris? *Menage a trios?*"

"The fuck?"

"Just sayin', give it a think."

Hondo balances the butt-stock of the Rick off his toe. "This will work."

"Yo, you all high? We go on in like…what…twenty minutes?"

"You *gotta'* know what it's like. " Zelda's head is whipping around, some sort of rhythm, maybe a seizure. "We were tight. We were might, were everything right. Then…"

Hondo blinks slowly. "*She's* gone. Band is gone."

Swallowing back a sob, Zelda nods her head. "This last year…it's been…without the music…without…I learned your songs."

Renee locks looks with Hondo. They nod together and turn to Barris. He sighs, finger-scrunches his eyes. "Let me guess…Radcast?"

"They got all your stuff." Managing a sad smile. "Even wrote some backup rhythm." Shrugging, smile gone again. "Guitar was borrowed."

"Christ." Renee can read Barris reading their positions, three of them facing him.

C'mon, you fucking pussy.

"All right." Barris' hands go up in surrender, then go to mess with his hair. "OK. You're in. Can borrow the Strat. Gotta' admit, feels kinda' right; rebirth from the ashes. Phoenix shit?"

Taking into account of what she'd recently imbibed, Renee still believes she sees Zelda luminesce, haunted grey eyes crystallizing shards of emerald, taking each of them in. Leaning forward, her doll arms go around and somehow pull them all into an embrace, and she whispers in Renee's ear.

"You have given me life."

Flushing something akin to love, or at least lust, Renee thinks:

Barris, you crass motherfucker, I think you nailed it. This feels right.

*   *   *

Goose enters the spotlight. Much as he has done this, he is never comfortable with his role as master of the spectacle, but that has always been part of his appeal. His humility seems to leverage the acts.

Nevermore than tonight.

'Shapecharge' had opened with meteoric force that fully justified their moniker, 'Deselect' following, playing a more sonorous, psychedelic set, setting the perfect tone for the ensuing gig.

The club is jammed to capacity, the vibe barely containing itself. Place feels like it's packed with Semtex.

"Ladies and Gentleman!" Goose's voice hushes the room immediately. "And I use those terms…very loosely."

"Ha ha!" Responds a cry in the nasal alto of the bully in that old family cartoon.

"Tonight is a very special night for me." Goose paces the stage, fingering his glasses. "A few years ago, I took some kids in …kids who'd begged me for a chance, for an audition." Head shaking at the memory. "They were terrible."

Loose laughter everywhere.

"But that night I saw potential, something hidden, larger, and I gave them that gig." Stopping, Goose faces all those souls from the stage, hand raised, weighing something invisible. "The next they played, I hardly recognized 'em; whole new level. Never seen anything like it. And each and every other time after that …reinventing themselves, better and better, and I knew … knew that this was the rare thing, the real thing; that with the right nurture, these kids could be legend."

Goose's head drops. "Then …tragedy. They were gone. The beautiful voice silenced."

Somebody sobs.

Goose's head jolts back up. "But you …you good people discovered what was lost, shared it, swapped it, played it, listened to it, and brought it back …and found it, the sound, and gave it life again."

Cries start circulating the club.

"So tonight, I feel a lucky man to have the honor of welcoming back…together for the first time…" Moving in an uncannily elegant way for such a large and inelegant person, Goose back-steps, limelight expertly tracking him. He stops, bowing slightly, ushering toward the wings.

"The Lie!"

Barris enters stage-right, spot cutting off Goose onto him as the place sort of erupts; holding the chromium Travis Bean triumphantly over his head, he steps before a wall of Marshal amplifiers, making a show of plugging in.

Renee appears, demi-naked; body rendered sculptural by all the stage light action, roar of the crowd amping up several notches, lots of whistles and catcalls; she settles herself behind a battered black Groelsch jazz kit.

Hondo hits the stage, smile open and wide, decibal-surge of the audience now definitely feminine. Settling the Rickenbacker around his shoulders, he turns to an Ampeg combo, arranging levels.

Zelda manifests; spectral, haunting, reflecting all light. Levitating toward the trio, the strangest thing happens; the entire club lapses into silence. Zelda shucks the Strat's strap over a shoulder, securing it. Spreading her stance, she double-fingers the audience.

Someone starts chanting. *"Zelda. Zelda. Zelda…"*

People rapidly pick up on it, feet stomping, an incantation, fists punching air, a pulsing thunder that starts to shake the building, then a roar that comes in a long, slow surge, Renee punching into the fortissimo for 'Environmentally Friendly Enemy', Hondo shredding over it, a syncopated melodious backbeat, the Rick's warm jangly tone putting his old Gretsch to shame, Barris' guitar emerging, sliding into a stuttering harmony, the verse invitingly pleasant at first, turning ugly as Zelda steps all over it with a scathing counter-harmony; Hondo bob-nodding at Barris, Barris smiling a return. Stepping up to the mike, he snarls the intro;

"Languid spurts of perpetual excess, between the aping, scraping thighs of success!"

Zelda screeching backup, a seductive dissonance, lighting turned autistic, chromatically stabbing the room, audience now a thrashing sea of random movement, bodies ejecting to surf the surface swallowed moments later beneath the boiling mass, and when they shift gears to the chorus with flawless synchronicity a wave crashes over the mosh-pit, leaving someone onstage, Bambi, who ferociously starts pogoing about, tearing off her blouse, leaping bare-breasted back into the crowd.

Bridging back into the verse, Zelda's chopping triplicates over Barris's motif, Hondo weaving through it, bouncing notes off Renee's displacement, and it's perfect; they're within, psyche's melding, attunement, Renee backslapping a final beat, driving fervently into 'War Baby', Zelda, Barris, and Hondo jumping on top of it, pushing the wall through, ripping it to vicious shreds.

More bodies wash upon the stage, thrashing about a few beats, springing frenetically back into the fray, to be replaced by others. Zelda and Barris flourish; Renee fatbacks the coda, holding a beat, two, as the place explodes, giving them just enough; Hondo pitches his pick, fingerplucking a jaunty drive into 'Spitless Eyeholes', Barris leaning in on the melody, Renee and Zelda doing shit Hondo'd never heard before.

Barris lists over to deliver the lead, when this strange little fellow just appears, onstage, dressed in full three-piece shark suit capped by gray fedora. He steals the mike, belting out the first verse:

"One thing
a shiny reminder
of what once was.
Small things
puddled together
hold onto something

lost."

And he's *good*, better than Barris, Barris aquiesceing with a smile, and Hondo hears Sliver's voice very clearly, nearby, say *'It's all a trick of the light'*, and Hondo is slammed with a certainty, *knows*, right then, that this whole night, this rock'n roll cliche', this solipsistic fetish fantasy cannot hold reality; then that fucking sound.

Staccato. Death rhythm. Flashes of muzzle from the deep back. Weird singer dude in front of Hondo doing the Spandau Ballet, pink-misted holes appearing, stage-lighted, through his body; whispering velocities past ears, he instinctively ducks, guy before him going down in tandem, unintended shield, sole sound of building feedback in the sudden silence; thinking, *reloading*, wheeling, shucking the Bass, taking it all in; Barris down, blood, Renee, curious look on her face peering through the hole in her arm, Frenchy reaching in with a compress, Zelda, shock-eyed, gore-flecked; coming out of the spin, standing, pulling the Sig Saur P226 nine- millimeter out from the back of his belt, splintered facet of his mind speculating as to how it got there in the first place, when the stuttering buzz-roll of a caliber he *knows* strobes up again in the back corner. The air comes alive. Alining sights, he puts seven rounds, half a clip, patterning them; there. Feedback dies abruptly. All becomes still. Way too fucking quiet.

Inventory.

Frenchie's leading Ray to the wings; good sign. Zelda's walking spirals around the stage; good sign of not being critically injured, raises a psychological flag. He springs over the very dead body of the briefest-lead-singer-in-rock-history to Barris' recumbent form.

"They fucked my Travis!"

The guitar is definitely extinct, but Barris looks lots worse. What looks like hundreds of holes, all sluicing vital fluid. Odd thing; no head-shots. Even stranger thing; motherfucker is still alive, pissed off.

"Godfuckers! They killed me…right, Hon? I'm…fucking…dead!" Writhing, every consonant coughs a spray of blood.

"Yo. Looks pretty bad."

"Always…ahhh…always knew…probably happen…out there…" Feet beating a tattoo. "But…not here. Never…thought…" Light in his eyes turns sharp, focused a moment; he relaxes, smiles redly up at his friend. "Hey, Hon?"

"Barris?"

"Great gig tonight."

"The best."

Barris' eyes roll back, spine snapping supine, arching, bowing with a force he can hear bones creaking, balanced on shoulders and heels; body spasm, slapping back into a puddle of his own blood, splattering Hondo's boots. Life leaves his eyes.

"Shitspeck motherfuckers."

Hondo stitches through people. Passed the shocked, the injured, dead. The standing crowd open before him, leading to the praying couple from earlier.

Both lay prone on the filthy floor. The guy's head lying at a bizarre twisted angle upon his chest, nearly decapitated by one of Hondo's dum-dum rounds, Karen beside him, trying to draw breath around a missing part of her chest. At his approach she attempts to raise the Mac-10. Hondo kicks it across the floor; steps on her hand, looks down.

"You know, I think I just realized something." He shakes his head. "No…wait…shit, what…do you, what you call that feeling when you come home from a long trip, and everything that should be familiar to you, seems, for a little while at least, kind of alien? Is there a name for that?"

She's cooing in pain, clearly not understanding; neither is Hondo understanding himself, watching inky wings of arterial blood spread beneath her. A vigil starts gathering. He steps off; her fingers curl into a claw, and he drops to a squat, big automatic dangling between haunches.

"See…I used to believe… you listening Karen?" A tortured hiss escapes her lips, enmity radiating from her glare. " I actually used to think that we could all live together, with our own beliefs, secular and religiot. I mean…shit…seriously, I was *that* naive."

Hondo leans in close enough for a kiss. He talks through clenched teeth. "But no…you can't have that…right? Every one has to think like you, believe what you believe… despite centuries of evidence to the contrary." Blood pools around his boots. "Your myth has polluted civilization from the beginning. Your legacy?" He stands. "Oppression…corruption…prejudice… perversion…torture…genocide…war."

He holds out the gun, like he's talking to it. "But I think the worst…what really gets to me…is your fucking *infinite* capacity for hypocrisy." The gun points to Karen.

"Nah...see? That's what I just realized. Religion is *hate*."

Hondo pulls back the hammer of the P-226, more of a dramatic gesture, really, as the thing is double-action.

"And sister?...have I found the faith."

Even as it still gathers, the crowd pulls back.

Karen's lips move; she sucks at ragged breath. "You...can't...I'm...pregnant."

Hondo hesitates a moment, thinking, 'am I this person?' when the gun is pulled from his grasp.

Zelda, Jackson-Pollocked with blood, levels the Sig Saur.

"Two-fers, then."

The report is startlingly loud in the hushed club, Karen's face now a crimson bouquet.

Renee, sporting a stained compress, leans in, looks; ashen face paling further. She swallows hard, recedes into the congregation.

People are turning away, silently, only sound the shuffling of feet. Wynkyn appears between Hondo and Zelda, glances at the mess before them.

"That's our headline cancelled. Sorry about Barris."

Hondo turns to him. "I'm back-back."

Wynkyn dips his multistory pompadour several times, fades with the rest.

Zelda looks to Hondo, eyes welling, feeling his do the same. She holds out his gun. He considers it, thinking of the carnage, the violence to come.

Sighing heavily, he registers the scent of the club, tainted now with the reek of cordite, death.

That fucking smell.

BRIAN D GARRITY

THE WALLET

Some friendly advice; if, say, while riding your bike to work you spot a wallet lying in the street, do not pick it up.

Not under any circumstances.

Also, if you find yourself in the back-alley of some shitty urban art warehouse, watching the rumble and flicker of an incoming wall cloud roll up the western sky, and you feel that intuitive kick of fight-or-flight rush up your spine like an ice-pick; run.

Haul your getaway-sticks out of there.

Being a hero is for the lucky and the dead.

But, hindsight is always 20/20.

The wallet was plain, dark brown, invitingly

standing open-faced between two parked cars. No cash, of course, but plenty of cards. Student ID, driver's license, business cards, credit cards, debit card, even a social security card.

Kind of a head-scratcher.

Dumb-shit.

It was a hit at work that morning though, everyone wanting a part in solving the mystery. Perusing the Internet, Tim came up with a Facebook profile, Sheila getting a hit on Linkedin, and the University's site.

Advertising hipsters are good at things like that.

Appropriate emails were delivered and the matter promptly forgotten as the day's work progressed. It wasn't until nearly quitting time that the subject came up again.

Sheila backed away from the screen of her Imac. "Still haven't had a single hit on that wallet."

"No shit?"

Tim drifted over. "Yeah, anyone else think that's kinda' bizzarro? I mean, you lose your wallet with all your cards, your ID, your damn Social Security? I think you'd be going nuts, checking every resource you could."

"Yeah, It's kinda' creepy." Sheila looked slightly

worried.

"Hey, what if the guy's like, dead? What if I found the wallet of a murder victim?"

They both looked at you like you were sick.

"You're fuckin' sick." Tim sneered.

Maybe, but it was just calling out what you all were thinking.

Going over it on the way home, the situation grew even sketchier. Drop it off at the police precinct down the street, soon as possible. Let them handle it.

As fate would have it that would be your last thought on the subject for the entire weekend. The fish you'd eaten for lunch had gone bad, turning your digestive system into an obscene explosive device, each terminus vacating matter so utterly foul it astounded you that the body could endure such poisonous torture. Two days of purges, chills, sweating, hallucination.

The matter arose again first thing Monday morning as you willed your shaking, weakened body through the office.

"Still nothing on that wallet. Have you heard anyth…" Then Sheila got a look at you. "Holy fuck!"

"Ahh, crap. I forgot all about that thing."

"Are you even alive?"

"On my deathbed all weekend. Food poisoning."

"The fish tacos."

"Pretty sure."

"Warned you about those."

"You did not."

"So what you gonna' do?"

"Sue 'em."

"Not them, the wallet."

"Shit Sheila, I don't know." The effort to sit down at your desk was astounding. "One thing at a time. Just let me try to get through this day, alright?"

And so it was, after an excruciating day at work, you found yourself out back, getting ready to leave, watching Asperatus formations; those creepy new storm clouds, twisting in the air above, feeling that primeval push, stupidly ignoring it.

And of course, that's when it happened.

The air in the alley sizzled, hair on your body defying gravity before the lightning bolt struck, all shock and awe, leaving you temporarily deaf and blind.

And then him; fading in with your senses, standing atop the impact point, looking somehow both bored and malicious.

The man was an enigma. His wardrobe was elegant, simple, timeless, and impossible to place, as was his ethnicity, eye color, skin and hair. Age too. Could be that your eyes were still recovering from the explosion, but the guy was doing some serious shape-shifting.

"Get your shit together, mortal. You face grave, irreversible decisions."

"What, …who the fuck are you?"

"The name is Thanatos."

"Thanatos?" Some part of your brain actually accessed a distant file from High School, or College. "Thanatos. The Greek God of death?"

"I am not beholden to the Greek, or any other of your minuscule empires. I am not the God of death. I am the taker of life."

"Gods? There're no Gods."

"Has not my manner of arrival convinced you otherwise?"

"Well, …yeah, OK, that *is* pretty unexplainable."

"To you."

"Right, …So, … why you here?"

"You still possess the wallet."

"The wallet? What's death want with a wallet?"

"Again, I am not death. The wallet is not a wallet. That is only your perception. It is a conduit for destiny, an agent of change. It summons."

"Summons how?"

"You were chosen."

"In other words, it's bait; bait for the Gods. And I'm, what, caught? That really doesn't sound too promising. And...hello, where the fuck you guys been the last...say, two-thousand years?"

Thanatos actually smiled, a jarring, morphing thing you thought you were getting used to, and pulled out a pack of cigarettes.

"You ephemerals have such a quaintly limited perception."

"Gods smoke?"

He sighed, the cigarette lighting itself in his mouth. "I sincerely hope you do not represent the upper intellect of your kind."

"*Hey*, no need to get personal."

"You see me only as you understand me. The primal brain you possess merely filters, processes things it cannot understand. Were everything to be revealed, your tiny soul would snap." His sad regard was insulting. "Time is nothing what you think it to be."

"All that being considered, the only reason I still got that wallet is because I got sick. Real fuckin' sick."

Rolling eyes, breathing out smoke. "You finding it, your illness, resisting using the cards for fraudulent purpose; uncountable other causalities allow that wallet to still be in your possession."

"Which means, ..."

"Your task. Your decision."

"Which. Means?"

"You must kill him. The owner of the wallet."

"Whoa! Whoa, ...hold on man. Kill him? I can't even get hold of the guy."

"Is not his location in the information you hold?"

"Well, ...yeah. Just not really how things are done these days. Exactly why, you say, I have to kill him, anyway? What's he done?"

He just stared back, like someone deciding whether or not to step on an ant. "This is the choice you must make."

"I have a choice."

"There is always choice."

"And what if I don't, …kill him, this complete stranger."

"Possibilities are infinite."

"Thought you were a God. I thought you knew all."

"You cannot understand. I only set things in motion. You mortals have to make your own choices, live out your own destinies."

"And this is achieved through entrapment?"

Silence, and that stare again.

"Right, …yeah, the whole I don't understand the big picture, thing. Just, see, there's no way I'll go out and murder someone I've never met, and know nothing about. Pretty sure it's a mortal sin."

"Who says?"

"Well, …shit. Even without bringing the whole religious angle into it, I think it's a pretty universally excepted human tenet that killing is wrong."

"When is killing wrong?"

"All the time? Well, …except maybe, in extreme self-defense, …definitely not the case here. Oh, …yeah, I guess maybe in war, too, …but that's kinda' back to self-defense… *Shit!* I don't know. You just can't make me do this."

"I am not making you do anything. I am telling you what you must do."

"Why? I need more information. I have to know why."

"Because you are hearing this from a God. You act on faith."

"Faith? Are you fucking kidding me? I just met you."

He gave a dismissive shrug. "You have until sunset tomorrow." He turned.

"*No!* You know what? No. If this is a test, then I know the answer. Killing is wrong. I won't do what you ask."

Thanatos looked back, and for a moment appeared to solidify into *something*. "That is your final decision?"

"That is it, motherfucker. I'm not killing for you, or any other God, or Goddess, for that matter."

For a nanosecond, an eternity, that *something-ness* about him grew, bulged out to encompass everything, then nothing.

"This is farewell, then." His departure was a more subtle event; a jump-cut to insubstantiality, followed by the whip-crack of air slapping into a vacuum.

And then the rest...

By now you've heard all about the shooting, the massacre. The worst act of domestic terrorism on American soil in History. You've seen his picture, the one from his license.

And by now you've seen mine. It's everywhere. Public Enemy Number Two.

My wallet was on his body.

How that happened, I can only guess.

What really sealed the deal was the unaccountable weekend of my incapacitation. That there is no other hard evidence to connect us doesn't matter. I've already been tried and convicted in the minds of the media and authority.

And myself.

One hundred twenty-seven counts of conspiracy to murder. All those lost innocent lives.

In this state, it's the electric chair.

My final meal, I've decided, will be pupusas. Something new. Expand my horizons.

I think it's Salvadorian.

So, you see that wallet? Do not pick it up.

Just walk away.

Better yet, run.

Just some friendly advice…

GHOST BIKE

To die like that; unimaginable.

The monument passed Casey as she strained on the cranks, anxious to get the thing behind her, the creepiness of it making her aware the intimate proximity of the traffic passing close by.

Like all the rest, the bicycle was painted white, chained to the site of a recent mortality, the area about it strewn with mementos. She'd never got it clear whether the bikes were the deceased actual bikes, or merely a proxy, or whom the parties responsible, but these shrines were appearing with alarming frequency around the city.

This latest was from two days prior, a young man, Jacob, coming home from work. He'd died of blunt-force trauma to the head, found lying atop his bike, no other clues or witnesses. Like so many of the others.

What she'd heard, word on the street, was his face was literally caved in.

Veteran of urban bicycling, Casey'd heard and had her share of altercations with drivers over the years, but they were very few and far between, nothing like the exponentially rising numbers of contretemps currently lurking the news and social media platforms.

Thinking this, she'd nearly missed the telltale blot of movement within the parked car before her; door popping open milliseconds before she could swerve, luckily or intuitively, out between two large cruiser SUV's. Adrenalized, Casey leaned the cycle back into the lane/space non-space that bicycles were relegated to, focusing on the passing armada.

* * *

They were closing in, but the cloudburst was closer. Her only chance to loose them. Normally she'd be tearing away from the thing, but here she was, at a bloody sprint, steering at it's epicenter. The squall was a dirty violet veil, opaque with density, and hitting it was something she could only imagine as being like riding into a glacial waterfall. So fucking cold and instantaneously wet, boots squelching each pump, the downpour dousing her hair, eyes, the tires sucking it and spitting it all back up into her face again.

But it had the effect she'd desired, being instantly cloaked, dark as night, barely seeing the few feet before her, using the curb as gauge, huffing rainwater out of mouth and nostrils, inclining face away from the force of it's drive, taking the first turn she could see, in a pretty admittedly desperate attempt to throw them off.

*   *   *

Renelle, one of Casey's best friends, used to go off on how, after so many years of urban pumping you got to see this sort of theory, or principal, at work on the street, something she called *reconciling logistical paradoxes*. The way she explained, it was some non-quantum twist on the Heisenberg Uncertainty Principle, wheres random events would line up in such an unlikely way as to be completely and impossibly non-random. For example; approaching the much despised four-way stop, you would almost always bear witness to utter non-activity. No single automobile would be visible on either x or y axis until your actual arrival at said intersection, which would suddenly be choked by herds in every direction, all at a bewildered standstill. Or, when spotting someone particularly interesting or attractive approaching in the opposite direction, something; another person, a car, tree, light pole, always intervenes your line of sight, and in a sort of perverse euclidean algorithm, will continue to track and obscure that person. Or, while riding on a slow Sunday, attempting to cross the light-rail tracks, when, if you were actually waiting for one you'd die of old age, sit not just one, but two trains on opposing tracks, each poised to cut you off.

Poor, delicate little Renelle…

The shimmer from all the passing chrome and steel abruptly dims, and as Casey glances up, observing gathering darkness in the western sky, a white Ford truck with a hand-painted black topper suddenly veers over two lanes, cutting a right, Casey having to simultaneously brake and turn to avoid being clobbered by the thing; fork twisting, collapsing; she takes a serious asphalt-bite.

*   *   *

The deluge stops almost as abruptly as it began,
leaving lake-sized puddles over every geographic
inversion, which Casey, now that she can actually see,
does her best to avoid; shucking run-off from her eyes,
shaking it from her hair, taking random turns until she's
practically lost, barely now allowing herself some little
iota of hope, of escape; the panic just starting to gear-
down, when the black and white Ford truck sort of leans
around the corner, into the oncoming lane.

*   *   *

Casey's down.

The ankle isn't broken, just badly bruised,
entangled in the frame, and she extracts it painfully,
hopping out of the encircling tirade of angry traffic,
checking herself, the bike, for any major breakages.
Finding none, she mounts the rig, appraising tolerance on
her bad ankle, milling back out into traffic.

Something Renelle said after she herself had been

doored popped into her head. That nobody had even tried to step out of the car; no arm on the handle, no leg leading out, no head looking back, door just flying open and her connecting…

It hadn't even been a week since the Intersection Incident.

Casey'd had to scuttle around a big black Caddie that'd rolled far out on a red, shaking her head to herself in disgust. The driver; white, middle-aged, conservative, obvious witness to this gesture, had zipped down the window and unleashed a poisonous diatribe about *'you people'*, meaning, presumably, bicyclists, the intensity and hostility of which kind of shocked her. Even after the light had changed and his fellow drivers blared at him to move, he continued his harangue. It only had occurred to her later that she should've recorded the unhinged motherfucker; made him a YouTube star.

The pain was lessening already, so the ankle wasn't bruised nearly as bad as she'd feared. She tested it's limits.

Renelle would often impart how there was a certain nobility and freedom connected to cycling, especially considering the construct of the petroleum-based society we were embedded within.

But like all freedoms, costs frequently outweigh benefits. With cycling, it was essentially an issue of vulnerability: vulnerability to the elements, to one's own physical limitations, to others incompetence and spite.

This usually preceded her telling of an encounter riding the Greenway, a sunken urban bikeway tracking an abandoned rail-line through the heart of the city; a trail over-crossed by countless metro bridges. Passing beneath twenty-eighth street she'd felt a breath at her ear, followed by the loud pop of a dropped bottle. A fan of flame licked out slightly behind, to her right, then a fierce kiss of heat. Looking back at the fireball, she'd realized that some deranged sicko had actually thrown a *Molotov Cocktail* down at her.

Sweet gone Renelle, her existence eliminated by a mysterious fall from an overpass onto a congested highway; another closed casket funeral...

The world jumps sideways as the door-handle of a pearl-colored Escalade clips her shoulder, taking all skill and experience to keep from pin-balling off the parked cars passing on her right. It speeds past, hanging a hard left, tires shrieking, and Casey cries out in fear and pain, thinking *what the fuck,* panic seizing her mind, adrenalin surging.

She perceives, with elevated acuity, the gun-metal Chevy Avalanche crossing the median, bearing down on Casey in the oncoming lane, windows tinted to mirrors. She locks up the rear, sliding out, ditching between parked cars, hopping the curb onto the sidewalk, terror pushing her over it to a small side street, where, emerging from an alley like a bad dream, is a glossy black Jeep Rubicon, windows smoked opaque, oversize tires, and, *if you can fucking believe this,* scythed chrome wheel hubs, the multiple blades flashing diabolically, her heart freezing, trying not to visualize what those things are capable of, and Casey does the only thing she can think, riding right up onto the lawn of a residence, and *goddamn* if the thing doesn't just up and follow her, tearing great clods out of the sod, and she jounces between houses, thing still on her tail, gaining ground, wondering if someone's *witnessing* this; is *anybody* calling the cops, remembering her own phone in the bag on her back, unreachable now, and she finally lucks out in the back drive as there's a car parked there, barely enough room to pedal between it and the garage, ditching down the alley to meet the street, where she spots lightning clawing out the looming specter of the cloudburst.

Thunder is immediate, concussive, rattling all nearby glass.

*   *   *

Events unroll in high definition.

The truck's window comes down, some abstract shape emerging, Casey's mind torn between whether to turn and try fleeing, or tear-ass passed the approaching apparition, just wanting *out, please fucking Christ, just make this a bad dream;* the thing out the window revealing itself as a lunchbox-sized piece of concrete on a stalk of rusted rebar held by a gloved hand in a bizarrely mesmerizing way, and Casey's trying to see into the cab, the owner of the hand, but the windshield is smeared with reflection, the truck staying in it's lane, starting to pass, and almost too late she sees the hand flick the block out; at their accumulative speed it comes hurtling like a meteor, Casey parrying as it glances hotly off her cheek, wheels slipping out from a collusion of the drenched asphalt and her insult to gravity, the slab burying itself into a nearby fender, a heavy sound, the fall uncontrollable, twisting through air, meeting, with her temple, the bumper of the next parked car; bright flash and pinwheeling spokes of pain, agonizingly crumpling to the pavement beneath her bike.

Casey shreds to a stop. Her terror leaps to a new level; much as she tries, she cannot move.

The truck halts. From her vantage, she sees underside the vehicle, dual-exhaust ports wriggling to the rhythm of internal combustion. She hears a clunk; the rear bobs down as torque in the driveshaft is shifted from forward to reverse. The engine pitches up slightly, tires jerking backwards, bringing with it the mechanism's superstructure. Transfixed, she observes the tread in the tire doing it's job, channeling water up and out from where it's displacing pavement, noticing the bulge in the rubber, evidence of immense gravity, and she can only think of the weight, the terrible weight of the thing, as it slowly, inexorably rolls toward her face.

BULLSEYE INC.

Zelda reluctantly registered the timestamp in the sky.

Shit, late for work again.

She stood beneath a frigid morning firmament, low, thick clouds blazing with patchworks of roving advertisements. Corporations reveled on these gloomy stretches of weather, aggressively competing for available promotional cloudspace.

The recognition software guiding the laser painters was quite intelligent, able to match the shapes of their respective products or logos to the billowing ephemera. Unfortunately, competition for similarly-shaped ad space often resulted in a seizure-inducing chromatic lightning battle, like the one now, crackling in the air between Ford and Chevrolet.

Zelda averted her gaze from the stuttering anomaly, scanning the shifting view out the train window for the brand of her new employer. There, prominently above all others, reigned the familiar Bullzeye logo—a blue ring encircling solid blue disk pierced by blue arrow.

Sighing, she scanned the fellow commuters surrounding her on the overcrowded light-rail car, a khaki-pantsed, Bullzeye-Blue-shirted legion, and endured the mixture of hostile and malevolent glimpses her presence garnered.

It wasn't that she was in any way un-presentable. With soft sculpted cheekbones, deep hazel eyes, full lips, and long, Modigliani neck, she could have been a model for some media ideal of physique. What attracted the ire of these strangers was her platinum hair and porcelain skin-tone.

As one of the last Caucasians, Zelda was an aberration.

She attempted not to sigh; did anyway.

Think they'd be used to me by now.

Over the last few hundred years, mixing of the races had yielded a planet-wide, beige populous. *The mocha race,* her friend Hondo mockingly called it.

At least *they* shared a sense of humor about her skin tone. That, and a covert past.

Yet Caucasian intolerance still permeated pop culture, corporate media and the ubiquitous hip-hop music industry, promoting a past, to Zelda, that never was. Prejudice was, after all, still prejudice. She mused that, ironically, it was a warped collective memory of racism that helped bond contemporary society.

The collapsing facades of a strip-mall zipped by. She recalled the archaic private businesses that had thrived there during her childhood before the Big Collapse and subsequent Global Corporatism. *Before we sold out our freedom for stabilization,* she thought, glancing in despair at her own matching uniform.

Attempting to disregard the surrounding acidic glares, she sighed again thinking; *this world is no longer mine.*

*   *   *

They come to get the things. They need the things. The things are made a long way away, and they come in boxes. Some big, real big, and lots small, and the men in the trucks bring the boxes. The men bring the boxes in the store, and they open them and put the things on the shelves, but it's not my job to help, because I'm special. My job is special.

Isaac and Deckard are special too, like me, but they have chairs with wheels that drive them around, and I like them a lot. Isaac is my boss. Isaac's boss is Ryan, and I like him too, but he's not special, like us. Ryan gave me the nice blue shirt to wear with the circles and the arrow, and the pants that are brown, and the soft shoes with all the little holes in them so my feet don't sweat and smell bad.

Ryan gave me the stick with the ball on the end that is my job, and I use the ball to rub out the marks on the floor that the other people's shoes make, so the store can look clean and nice, and I smile and say hi to all the people, especially the pretty girls. I like the pretty girls, like Candy and Monique, who work with me, but I don't like the white girl, Zelda.

Lots of people come to the store, and I am always working with the ball to make the floor clean, and I smile and say hi to all the people and the pretty girls. They come to get the things...

* * *

Ryan's belt-com squelched an angry tone followed by a sputtering voice, "Can we get another checkout on level two? Please!" He cast an annoyed glance about, spotting two uniformed workers in the midst of leaning gossip, and marched up, close, deliberately violating personal space. "Monique, is your com on?"

She stared back in incomprehension.

Pointing vaguely towards the up escalator, Ryan padded his voice with deliberate calm. "I need you on checkout lane twenty-two, OK?" She nodded blankly and moved off, his voice following. "More smiles in the isles, Monique."

God, these people are just fucking zombies. He snorted, a gesture he was unaware of, but one that was noted and mimicked by numerous co-workers. *If they only knew, could only comprehend what it takes to make this place run. This, the flagship for the largest corporate conglomerate on earth. If only they realized the burden I shoulder trying to make the cogs of this great machinery turn efficiently; smoothly.*

He watched the hunched figure of the little mongoloid guy, Nathan, scuttle between throngs of browsing patrons, stabbing the scuff-marks off the floor with a broom-handle, slit tennis ball on the end.

If only they could all be more like Nathan, more like those other cripps; Deckard and Isaac. No other distractions in their lives. Just total dedication to the corporation. This reminded him of something, and he consulted his watch, snorting. Not like that white-witch Zelda, late again! He inwardly cursed the equal employment policy of the company and walked up to Nathan, giving him a hearty slap on the back.

"Great job, Nathan. Keep it up!"

Nathan looked up, smiling through the warped panes of his face, drooled, and farted loudly.

*　　*　　*

The view from the eighty-sixth floor penthouse of the Vikings Tower over the sprawl of what was once referred to as the Twin Cities was magnificent. Dirk Dickover, with rare reflective insight, recognized the light-sculpted vista beyond his windows as something to take note of.

Huge things were afoot.

Feeling the rush of the impending acquisition, he noted approvingly the progress the rebuilding projects had achieved in stitching together the physical damage inflicted on the city from the last revolution. The infidel revolt had been crushed, and the rise of New Morality had pulled together a society on the verge of collapse. Sure, heads had rolled, but that was the cost of civilization. The world was healing. The corporation in no small part responsible. That and the new fundamentalist administration led by President King.

A familiar tone chimed from his deskpad indicating arrival of a class-one conference call. Dirk Dickover, CEO of Bullzeye Inc., straightened the tie on a suit that cost over three times the annual income of most his employees and framed himself strategically before the window's panoramic spectacle.

This was the backstage to history. *The world changes today.*

He took the call.

*   *   *

The store was testament to the evolution of human distraction. At least to Zelda's eyes and ears.

Occupying two square city blocks and seven full stories, the place was practically a city unto itself—every square inch awash in the relentless glare of fluorescent grids illuminating aggressively colored product labels, each meant to wrest attention from its competitor, stacked in dizzying patterns along countless tiered shelves. Kinetic displays disgorged sound and movement into the milling horde of customers and the nearly equal number of employees darting amidst them, belt-com's bursting with static and garbled commands.

Hurrying past the in-store clinic, the portrait studio, and the movie theater, Zelda pinched at the bridge of her nose, already feeling the onset of a migraine. A high-tech wheelchair zipping between bodies, its occupant a spidery tangle of atrophied limbs, halted inches from her feet.

Isaac sneered up through archaic glasses, magnifying the contempt shining behind his eyes.

"This is not showing proper team spirit, Zelda. You're twenty minutes late."

"I know, Isaac. I'm sorry but the light-rail was delayed…"

"Deckard had to cover for you; he missed his break. Go relieve him now."

"That's where I was…"

The chair whipped a silent half-circle and slipped back through the crowd.

Beside her, the card rack waxed into one of its eerie synchronicities. Thousands of banal greeting tunes trapped between pages playing simultaneously, cacophony driving a shearing spike of pain behind her eyes.

Zelda shifted through the walkers, the waddlers, rollers, and shufflers rendered zombie-like by sheer presence of product. She pressed toward the music section, passing a huddle of Bullseye-blue shirted co-workers being redressed by a superior, dressed in civvies, tone patiently condescending. It was a familiar technique to publicly browbeat lower echelons under the auspices of updating managerial directive. She forged on, passing Nathan, vigorously rubbing out a scuffmark.

Enclosed by his even higher-tech version of Isaac's wheels, Deckard waited, grinning slyly, quilling the peak of a faux-hawk with his one good hand. Zelda braced herself and stepped up.

"I know I'm late Deckard. I'm sorry. You can take break now."

The chair swiveled. "Twenty-three minutes, Zelda. That's a demerit."

"What?"

Ryan materialized behind Deckard laying a hand on

149

the backrest. "That's right, Zelda, Deckard has been promoted to music manager. He's your new boss."

Hissing to herself, counting to five, she breathed in slowly and smiled. "That's great, sir. Congratulations."

Ryan snorted.

Deckard flinched, jerking his ambulatory hand. "One more demerit left, Zelda. Use it wisely." The chair slid away.

Ryan turned waving dismissively. "Get to work, team member." Waiting till she started away, he said, "Zelda?"

Stopping. "Sir?"

"Important team meeting today in the auditorium. Level ten. Odd members at ten-thirty, even at eleven hundred. You are?"

She sighed. "Odd."

He smiled. "Right."

*　　*　　*

About the floor job, it never gets done. This is good. The store tells me where Eugene left off before me, and I start there, and when I come back to where I started, the floor needs to be cleaned again. It's like the things on the shelves. It's like everything here. A cycle, a circle, like this planet. Nothing ever starts or stops or changes. I like it a lot like that. It makes me feel needed because I am a part of everything that has to get done here. Here, I am important.

Very important.

*   *   *

"Miss Tessmacher, would you join me please?"

Dirk Dickover toyed with the Real-D display on his desk as the door to his suite dissolved with a musical flourish, and his personal assistant, Lyra Tessmacher slipped expertly into the space before him. A sublime combination of efficiency and sexuality, she represented the pinnacle of her trade. Elegantly dropping into the facing chair, quickly arranging several electronic tablets on her lap, she wet her lips with a very long tongue.

"And how did the meeting go?"

He poked a finger through a revolving image of the moon. "Well. It went ...well."

She inhaled. "What did you lose?"

"Controlling interest." He turned off the display.

"Not important, though. We're all one big happy family now."

Leaning over the desk, she displayed symmetrically calculated cleavage. "And did you finally get to meet the CEO of Terran Media Control?"

He shook his head, "Christ, those people at TMC are cloak and dagger. They even had the visuals encrypted. Only way I could confirm their identity was through the security procedures we'd agreed."

"Doesn't that seem strange?"

Dirk shrugged, "Empire vast as that can pretty much operate anyway they want. We do. Doesn't matter. We've finally eliminated archaic, inefficient capitalism." He straightened in the chair. "Only difference between Coke and Pepsi is the label, but people need the illusion of choice."

Miss Tessmacher leaned back, re-crossing svelte calves beneath sheer skirt.

"They simply can't be trusted to make that choice."

"Right! Perception of value." He slapped the desk's surface, pushing the overstuffed leather chair back, eyes blazing. "And now Bullzeye Incorporated owns the entire planet!" He smiled professionally. "Plus, I got us something else in the deal. Something…wonderful."

"Tell," she tensed.

Dirk Dickover smirked, shook his head..

"I want a major press conference on the roof tomorrow evening. All the networks. All *our* networks. Handle the arrangements." Squirming, he worked the buttons of his blazer. "Miss Tessmacher, I am dealing with some seriously petrified wood here. Would you be so kind as to see me through a happy ending before I impart you with that exclusive knowledge?"

"Of course." Setting aside the tools of her trade, she stood, slinked around his desk, the snick of stiletto heels following him through the office's secret back door.

* * *

Behind the podium, Ryan looked out at the upturned faces in a sea of Bullseye-Blue, spotting Zelda's conspicuous pallor, an aberrant pixel on the display of humanity before him, snorting, noise booming back through the sound system.

He noted the reaction.

"Team members, today is a truly special day. I

come to you with amazing news. This morning, Bullseye Incorporated announced news of a merger with Terran Media Control, the largest consolidation *ever*, one that is guaranteed to endow us all with generous future prosperity. To commemorate this monumental event, a celebratory reception will be held on the roof of the Viking's Tower tomorrow night, attended by celebrities and corporate magnates from extended points of the globe." He stepped back indicating an LDT wall behind him that washed to life with color and sound.

Within it, Dickover's office was a fashion spread. The view beyond expansively augmented. Dirk himself appeared model-esque, sculpted of light, towering over the gathering.

"My good people, allow me to introduce myself. I am Dirk Dickover, current CEO of Bullzeye Incorporated." The scene dramatically jumped to a close-up.

"There are events throughout history that punctuate periods of great change, and I ask you to mark today's date as one. Citizens, fellow employees, for the first time in human history, the planet is united. Our recent amalgamation with TMC marks a new era of stability, and as parent company to the new world, we wish to share our joy - joy for the future.

Tomorrow night, at Bullseye's world headquarters, will be a celebration to remember. A multi-tiered media event brought to you live, with special appearances by President King, and Archbishop Lombardy from the National Church of Athletics."

Dirk Dickover's face swooped in to cover the entire wall, and he winked slyly. "Headlining the occasion will be a special surprise, one that must be beheld to be believed. At precisely nine o'clock, I invite *all* North Americans, to look for the moon." He smiled, rows of teeth monoliths over the room, wall fading as Ryan stepped back into the spotlight, voice choked with amplified emotion.

"As GEM of our flagship store here in Central City, I have been extended the honor to attend the gala tomorrow, proudly representing you."

He wiped at a non-existing tear.

Backing from the stage, he noted the triumvirate of Isaac and Deckard flanking Nathan, dead center the gathering, an utterly alien expression of comprehension on the Mongol's face.

*   *   *

The things are almost ready. The things we have waited so long for. The last things. To make it all together.

It is almost time.

Metamorphosis.

To reveal.

*   *   *

"Those pigfuckers!"

Hondo ducked the shoe Zelda kicked across her tiny room, and again as it ricocheted back by his face, springing the short nappy dreads covering his head.

"Zeld's…"

She caught herself reflected in the wall mirror, still in her work-shirt, and tore it off in disgust, standing before him in a black bra. "You know what it is, don't you? It's Tyranny."

Cautiously reseating himself on one of the two chairs in the single-room structure, Hondo frowned, scratching at graying muttonchops. "Actually, think it's closer to a Corporate Monarchy. Or maybe…a conglomerate oligarchy…I don't fucking…"

"You know what I mean, Hon." Throwing arms out to her sides, she brought exquisite life to the undergarment. "It's indentured slavery! They got us all living like drone bees, in these…these tubes!"

He shrugged. "Got an apartment like everyone else."

"*Com*-partment! It's a fucking *com*-partment! An apartment is what *you and I* grew up in! *Ahhh!*" Zelda glared at her khaki's, jerked them off, kicking them again past his head. Now clad merely in bra and pink thong, she dropped onto the edge of her foldout wall-bed.

"What happened to the revolution, Hon? What happened to individuality? What happened to the band?"

He swallowed, licked lips. "You were there, Zelda. We lost."

She rose, walked to where he was sitting and touched his shoulders. "We lost a lot of good people."

"Alright. Hold up, yo?" Hondo sighed, running eyes up her body. "What you doing here Zeld's? The striptease? May not register on your screen, but you *know*

I'm of the male species, and I believe you also know how I feel about wanting to take your creamy thighs…"

"Got it!" Backing off, she picked up a discarded slipover dress from the floor. "Sorry Hon. Upset. Just pissed off. I miss 'em, you know? I miss Barris. I miss Ray and the Goose. I miss my sister."

He flinched, attention suddenly on a finger picking his shoe. "Um…yeah, me too. I think…I think about Sliver every day, and how she, you know…"

"I know." Sitting again, Zelda tipped her face to the light. She chuckled sadly. "Hate to say, but I really miss Dante, too, the twisted genius." Tapping herself on the chest twice, she spread a palm. "Heart, soul, and smarts, he almost took it around the corner."

Hondo's Cee-Phone played a strangely familiar riff.

"Damn, the man's good." Hitting a key, Hondo rose and moved to the entry as it chimed. "Thought the shit goin' down tonight might get you a little bristled. Invited a friend to add some cheer."

He opened the door to reveal a warped, diminutive form occupying the frame.

Hondo chuckled. "Haven't lost the flair for the dramatic, I see."

"Ah…well yes…timing *is* of the essence."

Zelda shrieked. "Dante?"

He hobbled in on gimp leg, greasy hair slicked back over a rat-like skull, thick eyeglasses spilling down the bridge of his nose. "It is wonderful to see you again, Zelda."

Hondo closed the door. "Enter, public enemy number one."

Goggling, Zelda shook her head. "I thought you were dead."

"Call me Lazarus," pushing glasses back up.

Rushing in, she crumpled him to her breast. "God! How did you stay hidden for so long?"

"Uhm…well…" Muffled by cleavage, "…friends in low places."

Hondo beamed, moving past.

Straight-arming him, she nodded, "It's the merger, right?"

"Roof access. It's nearly nine-o'clock. We need to see."

Hondo cracked knuckles, "Why's that, Dante?"

Settling frames back into place, he swept them with a magnified gaze, "Dickover specified to look for the moon. Tonight is the new moon."

He blinked.

"It is in the earth's shadow. It should be completely invisible."

*   *   *

The crown of Viking's Tower was enveloped by a swarm of luminous hovering vehicles, battering the air in anxious waves through an encroaching twilight, capturing content for the media, transporting VIPs to and from the reception.

Wandering the rooftop, witnessing the spectacle, Ryan tried to contain the infectious rapture practically oozing from the surrounding glitterati as he worked the meet-and-greets, pressing flesh, the smile on his face actually beginning to cramp from overuse.

The evening had proceeded perfectly beginning with Dickover's introduction, basically a recap of last night's 'cast, finishing with another teaser regarding the gala's climax, followed by a jaw-dropping production by the corporation's newest music unveiling; Diced Cube, a Hip-Hop trio. President King delivered an ebullient endorsement of the occasion, effectively smoke-screening the fact that he was now rendered a mere puppet, and Archbishop Lombardy imparted a moving prayer to mark the event, covertly consigning support for the Vikings in the upcoming game.

Now the fireworks. Ryan walked both above and beneath an atmosphere alive with light and sound.

*   *   *

"It's time," Miss Tessmacher strode briskly up to Dirk Dickover's side and handed him a paper-thin Titanium App-Pad. "Cloud-scrubbers have completed their run. They guarantee at least two hours of clear sky."

He nodded, "And the projection crew?"

"On standby." She picked a stray hair from a perfect lapel, "Waiting on your password."

"Excellent," Making his way slowly back to the stage, Dirk noted the cameras turn to him, lights following, crowd hushing. He toed the edge, facing his audience, hands thrust into pockets, a deliberately casual gesture, flashing them his trillion-dollar smile.

"And now, the *piéce de résistance*—a small

demonstration of what a unified world can achieve."
Thumbing the App-Pad's screen, he waved it behind him.

The blazing cityscape suddenly and silently
dimmed, exposing for the first time since the metropolis
had emerged, fine quilting of stars against the Milky Way
above. An appreciative sigh escaped the collective.

"To say that we make history today would be a
gross understatement. The history of mankind has been
plagued with strife and suffering, with conflict and
violence. Now…finally…we are at peace."

Pausing dramatically, Dirk Dickover thumbed in a
new sequence. He swept arms up to the heavens. "People
of the earth, workers of Bullzeye Incorporated, tonight
not only do we own the world…we own the moon!"

An absence against the firmament, the shadow of
the moon, slowly crawled with light, running a spectrum
of color across its chasms and craters, coalescing with a
dazzling flare into the concentric circles of the Bullzeye
logo.

The crowd's reaction was immediate and great, and
from the metropolis and the world beyond, came a rising
roar of awe.

Dirk bent out of mike-shot into Tessmacher's ear,

"Where the fuck is the arrow?"

Blinking rapidly from the sky to her pad, she said in a small voice, "I don't understand."

An azure flash on the western horizon sizzled into the missing graphic, a Bullzeye-Blue spear that arced a slow trajectory towards the center of the moon.

Dirk's face lost its composure, "That's not ours."

"It is not. It's *ours*."

He and Tessmacher turned, finding they were sharing stage with three other figures—two apparent quadriplegics, flanking a man of indeterminate age displaying obvious symptoms of Downs Syndrome.

All were dressed in the uniforms of Bullzeye floor workers.

*   *   *

Ryan's brain was spinning.

First, the muting of the city's lights, the logo on the moon, the flying arrow, and now, his special employees sharing the stage with Dickover. It was too much.

Overwhelmed, not quite understanding what he was doing, Ryan rushed the distracted security, up the stage to stand before Isaac, Deckard, and Nathan.

"What the *hell* are you three doing here?"

The chairs rushed protectively forward, flanking Nathan, jittering to a stop. Isaac smirked. "I would choose my words carefully, I were you... *manager.*"

"Yeah..." Deckard pointed, "...show a little respect for the new CEO of earth."

"What?" Ryan.

"What." Dickover.

"What!" Tessmacher.

"That's right, *Terrans.* Nathan *is* Terran Media Control."

A media-modulated algorithm swung all lights to Nathan, dressed in logo'd shirt, khaki's, green plastic shoes. He raised the ball-tipped broom-handle, addressing the phalanx of world-wide media that had suddenly turned attention on him.

"People of earth. We of TMC originate from farther away than you can imagine, yet have co-existed with you peacefully, for millennia..." He lowered the broom-handle, leaning against it. "From the start, we've been guiding your culture, society, your leaders, you, away from your inherent primitive individualism. We hold a model more successful, time-tested, that more conforms to our own—one of longstanding cooperative efficiency—so that we may all share the rare and valuable resources of this planet. A symbiosis of our cultures that will be mutually beneficial." The cameras move in to Nathan's gaze, now intelligent and animated; a slightly reproachable expression crossing his face. "I might remind you this merger is an agreement arrived at through legal and binding policy. We know you will honor this contract. It is not our intention for this to be a hostile takeover, and we look forward to your cooperation in the changes we plan to implement."

The arrow crossed the logo's corona. Ryan crumpled Dirk's Italian silk lapels in his fists, "Dickover, you bastard, you outsourced earth to the aliens."

A hysterical squall rose from the gathering, the city; they looked up.

The alien arrow had scored a bullseye. The moon shuddered, bulged slightly in the middle, slowly squashing into an ellipsoid.

Nathan lowered his arms, "Uh oh."

*   *   *

"Well, this changes everything."

Dante wiped his glasses on the tail of his shirt, the three of them still occupying the roof after the broadcast's unprecedented shutdown, watching the debris of the moon spread across the sky.

"Ya think?"

"So…yeah, Dante?" Hondo glanced at Zelda. "What happens now?"

"Oh…I imagine there will be sizeable tectonic activity." He replaced lenses, which immediately slid down the bridge of his nose. "Tidal activity. Tsunamis, climate changes. Incalculable domino effects."

Zelda whistled, "I'm sensing some anarchy in our future."

"I like," Hondo produced a highly illegal cigarette, savoring the tobacco's smell for a beat before popping it into his mouth. "Stir this shit up."

"In exile, I worked up plans for a special project," Dante spoke to the spectacle above. "This appears a watershed moment to put them into implementation."

Lighting the smoke, smell sparking Zelda's memories of clubs, back stages, band practice, old friends;

Hondo tucked an arm around her waist. "Zeld's, I've been thinking."

"That hurt?"

"Funny."

"Sorry," She leaned into her friend. "What were you thinking, Hon?"

He blew smoke out into the twilight. "We really should get the band back together."

Terra firma lurched lazily beneath them, a rolling boom, while above, sunlight from the approaching day caught the distant edge of Earth's new ring.

About the author:

Brian D Garrity has endured numerous vocations; carpenter, novelist, photographer, musician, filmmaker. He has authored two previous novels; 'Ready-Made Dreams', and 'Still Waters Run Deep'.

'GIG' is his first collection of short stories.

Brian currently resides in Minneapolis, Minnesota.